**'I'm not...I ca** **Helen shrilled.**

'Not even if it means you'll be safe to go to see your son?' Noah prompted in a husky voice.

'I...' The words she had been about to speak froze as she remembered Nash, and her last-minute doubts seemed petty and foolish when a young, innocent child's safety and happiness were at stake. She would even contemplate marrying the devil himself if it meant being able to see Nash again, and Noah Kincaid was a long way from being satanic.

**Josie Metcalfe** lives in Cornwall now with her long-suffering husband, four children and two horses, but, as an army brat frequently on the move, books became the only friends who came with her wherever she went. Now that she writes them herself she is making new friends, and hates saying goodbye at the end of a book—but there are always more characters in her head clamouring for attention until she can't wait to tell their stories.

**Recent titles by the same author:**

VALENTINE'S HUSBAND
A WISH FOR CHRISTMAS
FOR NOW, FOR ALWAYS
WORTH WAITING FOR
LOUD AND CLEAR
FORGOTTEN PAIN

# HEART
# SURGEON

BY
JOSIE METCALFE

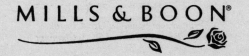

MILLS & BOON®

*First published in Great Britain 1997*
*Harlequin Mills & Boon Limited,*
*Eton House, 18-24 Paradise Road, Richmond, Surrey TW9 1SR*

© Josie Metcalfe 1997

ISBN 0 263 80123 3

*Set in Times 10 on 12 pt. by*
*Rowland Phototypesetting Limited*
*Bury St Edmunds, Suffolk*

03-9705-48207-D

*Printed and bound in Great Britain*
*by Mackays of Chatham PLC, Chatham*

# CHAPTER ONE

'ALL right, my little sweetheart,' Helen crooned as she taped the nasogastric tube in position. 'Nearly finished.' The tiny child squirmed weakly under her ministrations, uttering sounds that reminded her of the mewling of kittens.

'Mia doesn't like that, does she?' said Mrs Lomax as she hovered protectively over her little daughter. Helen glanced up and caught the sympathetic grimace on the young mother's face, and smiled reassuringly.

'It's a good sign when she starts complaining,' she reminded the mother. 'A week ago she was too poorly to care what we did to her.'

'A week ago I thought I was going to lose her,' Mrs Lomax said bleakly, and Helen knew she was remembering how desperately ill Mia had looked when she'd been wheeled out of Theatre after her surgery.

The frail scrap of humanity had sported a dressing taped to her chest almost from the base of her neck to her umbilicus, and had had so many leads and tubes attached to every portion of her anatomy that she'd looked like a kitten caught in a tangle of wool.

'She's still got so many things connected to her.' Mrs Lomax bit her lip, as though trying to hold back the words, but they emerged anyway. 'It feels as if she isn't mine any more,' she burst out as tears filled her eyes. 'I can't hold her or take her for a walk—I can't even feed her!'

Helen's hands kept moving automatically as she

5

finished noting down the figures on the various monitors, her eyes averted as she allowed Mrs Lomax a couple of seconds' respite with a large handkerchief.

She'd coped with such outbursts many times since she started nursing and had learned early on that every person coped in their own way—Mrs Lomax preferred to drag herself together without undue attention.

'Sorry about that,' she sniffed with a final mop at her reddened eyes. 'Every time it happens I feel such a fool.'

'No need to apologise,' Helen reassured her with an understanding smile. 'I've always believed that it's better to get it off your chest than to let it chew away at you from the inside.'

'I know that, but it's still not fair for me to take it out on you,' she muttered shamefacedly.

'My shoulders are broad enough to take it,' she teased. 'Anyway, Mia's not being ventilated any more and she doesn't even need the extra oxygen, so she's really doing well. What do you say we celebrate with a cup of hospital coffee?'

The offer garnered the expected wry laughter as Helen led the way to the opposite side of the unit, her eyes flicking from side to side as she passed the other bays to check on all her little charges and their worried parents.

As soon as she'd spent enough time with Mrs Lomax to have her back on an even keel she'd visit each of them, not because she didn't trust her staff but because it was one way of making sure that she filled every second of her time—to stop herself thinking.

If she sat down and allowed herself to think she might be tempted to take her own advice to Mrs Lomax to get her problems off her chest, and she had a horrible feeling that her scream of frustration would be heard right through the hospital.

It was nearly an hour before she finally made her way into the small glass-walled cubicle she called her own and found that, in her absence, a small mountain of paperwork seemed to have accumulated for her to deal with.

'I *must* get the job,' Helen muttered anxiously as she allowed her primary worry to surface briefly. There were several items of internal mail in the heap, and she swiftly scanned them for a likely-looking envelope. 'I've come too close to fail now, and time's running out. . .'

Her shoulders slumped when she realised that there was just the usual selection of documentation, updates and memoranda, and she sighed. It was all very well knowing that so far she had achieved every goal she had set herself, but if she failed at this final stage it would mean that the rest had all been for nothing.

All the pain she'd endured for the months it had taken to rebuild her life; all the endless hours of conscientious effort to work herself up to the top of the tree in her new specialty—well, she temporised, nearly the top. All she needed was this appointment. . .

It was hard to start the early shift at St Augustine's, knowing that at any moment a letter might be delivered—and she wouldn't even know it was there; wouldn't be able to open it until she got back to her cramped flatlet and found it.

Why was it taking so long for them to let her know? It seemed like several centuries since she'd put in her application. It wasn't as if she lived and worked miles away—the job she desperately wanted was based in this very hospital. . .

'Good morning, Sister,' a deep voice greeted her, breaking into her preoccupation as she stared down at the paperwork.

'Oh!' She jumped, startled by the unexpected presence of the tall figure in her office. Her heart thumped. How could she not have seen him, standing to one side of the window overlooking the ward? He was far too imposing a man to be overlooked. 'Good morning, Mr Kincaid. Can I help you?'

She was glad that she was sitting down when she felt the slight quiver in her knees at the thought that he might have come in person to give her the news about the job she wanted so much. After all, it was his specialised team she had applied to join. . .

'I hope so,' he said, his pleasant smile revealing even white teeth as he propped one lean hip on the corner of her desk and swung his foot in idle arcs. 'I'm hoping you're free this evening to join me for a meal. Would seven o'clock suit you?'

For several seconds Helen's brain was paralysed with shock at the unexpected invitation. She'd been working with him ever since she transferred to St Augustine's and he'd never spoken to her in anything but a professional capacity; never done more than smile absent-mindedly when she handed him a patient's file or a cup of coffee. Yet here he was, genuinely smiling at her for the first time.

She was still trying to come to terms with his sudden change of attitude as her thoughts began to whirl suspiciously. What was going on? *Why* was he asking her out? And why now?

'I'm afraid I don't go out,' she replied coolly, as she always did when anyone suggested anything resembling a date. She reached for the closest pile of paperwork, hoping that the tremor she could feel in her fingers wasn't as obvious as she feared. 'But thank you for asking,' she added, knowing that her insincerity could be heard in her tone.

'You don't go out?' he repeated questioningly, and out of the corner of her eye she saw his swinging foot suddenly grow still. 'Any particular reason?'

Helen silently cursed her unruly tongue.

She knew exactly how sharp Noah Kincaid's mind was, and her unguarded words had obviously been enough to set him wondering.

Well, he could wonder all he liked—there was no way that she was going to tell him about the disastrous mess she'd made of her life, or the tragic consequences of her actions. Just because he had suddenly decided to notice that the person he'd been working with wasn't a sexless robot. . .

Her disappointment that his visit hadn't had anything to do with the job she wanted so much lent an added touch of venom to her reply.

'You mean, apart from the fact that I don't have the time, energy or the inclination to play games any more?' She forced herself to meet his dark blue eyes without flinching, an inexplicable disappointment filling her that he was turning out to be just like all the rest. Until today she'd begun to believe that he was one of the few men in the world she could respect.

'Games?' he queried softly, the word a definite challenge. 'Explain.'

'Oh, come on!' Helen threw her pen down in disgust as she felt the heat spread across her cheek-bones. 'I've been working here for several months now, and the first time you invite me out is when I've applied for a position on your team. Is this the hospital version of the casting couch?'

The silence between them grew until it was almost palpable, while Helen's pulse raced frantically at the base of her throat. Her eyes were mesmerised as she saw his expression change, the unexpectedly boyish smile wiped off his face as though it had never existed.

Her breath froze in her throat as he straightened from her desk and drew himself up to his full height, his lean six-foot-plus body towering over her as she sat skewered to her seat by the force of his chilly gaze.

'Actually,' he said at last, 'it was more in the nature of an invitation to join the rest of the team for a meal to help you to start fitting in with us, but if you've decided to withdraw your application. . .?'

Oh, God! What had she done? a little voice wailed inside her head as her heart sank like a stone. What on earth had possessed her to make such an accusation against the one man in the world she wanted to impress? Why had she leapt to such unfounded conclusions when all he'd been doing was letting her know she'd got the job?

'Well?' he demanded brusquely. 'What's your answer?'

'Actually, I've got a question to ask before I can give you an answer,' she began shakily, pressing both palms to her desk to help her knees to bear her weight as she rose from her seat. He would still be a head taller than she was when they were both standing, but she saw no reason to give him the psychological advantage of looming over her seated figure.

At this precise moment she needed every bit of help she could get if she was going to retrieve the terrible situation she had created.

'Well?' he barked.

He'd had to take a step back to allow her the space to stand up but he was still so close that he seemed to fill her field of vision, his folded arms tightening the dark fabric of his suit jacket over his broad shoulders.

Her eyes travelled up the taut column of his neck to his face in time to see him raise one eyebrow, the dark blond crescent almost meeting the unruly strand of sun-streaked hair which permanently disobeyed all his efforts to subdue it as it curved across his lightly tanned forehead.

She drew in a deep breath and raised her chin a notch.

'Can I take it that this is my official notification that I've been offered the position on your team?' she demanded, schooling her voice not to betray the sudden surge of hope spiralling through her. She longed to be able to cross her fingers as she waited for his reply but, more than ever, she needed her hands to keep her upright.

'What?' He blinked in apparent surprise, and his forehead furrowed into a deep frown. 'Of course, it... The decision was made... You mean you haven't heard anything yet?'

'Not until this moment,' she confirmed with an extra tilt of her chin. 'There was nothing in my post at home this morning and, as you saw, I've only just arrived on the ward.'

'In which case, please accept my apologies,' he offered gruffly, and she saw a hint of colour darken the planes of his cheeks as he straightened up sharply to his full height. 'Obviously, I was under the mistaken impression that you'd been informed of the offer of the position.'

'Then the job's mine?' she demanded, almost breathless with elation.

'If you still want it,' he confirmed with more than a hint of discomfort as he stepped back from her desk. 'I can understand how you might have misinterpreted my invitation. . .'

'*If* I want it!' She broke in, unable to control the delighted chuckle which bubbled up in her throat. She had to fight down the urge to fling her arms around him and drag him around the cramped office in a dance of victory. 'Of *course* I want it. It's what I've been working towards for. . .ages,' she finished lamely, suddenly realising just how much she was in danger of revealing.

'Well. . .good,' he murmured faintly, as though taken aback by her fervent reaction. 'Does that mean you'll be free to join the team this evening? It will give you the chance to pick Sophie's brains before she finally leaves us.'

'I'd be delighted,' she agreed with a wide smile. 'Seven o'clock, you said?'

'Exactly.' He turned to make his way out of the cramped room, then turned back to pull a folded piece of paper out of the inside pocket of his jacket. 'This is the address of the place we're meeting,' he explained as he placed it gently on the top of a wire basket of paperwork with a wry half-smile before he strode out into the corridor.

Helen was flooded with euphoria that the job she'd coveted for so long was really hers. For one horrible moment she'd thought that she'd ruined everything, but. . .

Suddenly, she sank back into her chair and, with a groan, covered her face with her hands.

What an idiot he must have thought her, first leaping to such uncomplimentary conclusions as to think that he would be guilty of such unprofessionalism and then agreeing to meet up with the team and confirming the time without asking about the venue. . . But who cared? Her happiness won out and excitement painted her face with pleasure.

She'd have all the time in the world, now, to show him that such momentary lapses in common sense were not normal for her.

She consoled herself with the knowledge that she was good at her job, and Noah Kincaid must know it or she'd never have been offered a place on the team.

Even the normal run of aggravations, such as the backlog of patients waiting for soft-tissue magnetic resonance imaging and a delay in the return of results from the lab, couldn't ruffle her feathers that day.

Now that the uncertainty was over she felt as if her feet hardly touched the ground, able to cope easily with whatever the day threw at her.

'So. . .did you come up with one of the big prizes on the lottery?' Anne Denton demanded when she finally managed to corner Helen after lunch.

'The lottery? No. Why?' Helen blinked at her colleague in genuine puzzlement.

'Well, something's put that broad grin on your face, and I'm not letting you escape until you tell me what it is.'

'Oh.' Helen smiled at the young staff nurse. 'I was just trying to think what to wear this evening. . .' She bit her tongue to still the words when she saw the avid interest flash across the young woman's face, and realised what she had blurted out.

'Oh-ho! Who are you going out with? He must be special to get you to change the habits of a lifetime. Any-one I know?'

'Mr Kincaid asked me to join. . .' She began, but never got to finish the sentence.

'*Kincaid!*' Anne squealed, before clapping a hand over her mouth and remembering to keep the volume down as she began her inquisition. '*Noah* Kincaid? You've been invited out by the sexiest man in the whole hospital?'

'You needn't make it sound as if I'm the last person on earth anyone would ask out,' Helen replied, stung by the degree of amazement in Anne's voice. 'Anyway, it's not as if it's really. . .'

'It's not that.' The staff nurse's face had flamed when she'd realised how her words could be taken. 'It's because he's even worse than you are.'

'Worse? In what way?' Helen was taken aback.

'Well, you've got to admit that in all the time you've been at St Augustine's no one's ever known you to accept a date.'

'I don't have a lot of free time,' Helen began defensively, but once again she wasn't allowed to finish.

'No. No. You don't get the point,' Ann Denton broke in impatiently. '*You've* been asked out by almost every eligible male on the staff here—and a few ineligible ones—but you've turned everybody down, whereas *he* doesn't even seem to notice when a nurse tries to climb inside his clothes with him. . .'

'Annie!' Helen was genuinely shocked.

'At one point, some of the staff even laid bets as to whether he preferred partners of his own sex but. . .'

'Good God, no!' The exclamation was dragged out of Helen. She might not be interested in Noah Kincaid as a partner for herself, but there was no doubt that she had never met a sexier or more masculine man—even though it had taken his presence in her office this morning to bring the point home to her.

'Oh, some of them will bet on two raindrops running

down a window,' Annie said dismissively, thankfully mis-understanding the reason for Helen's surprise. 'But, as far as Noah's concerned, he's been here nearly three years and, as far as anyone can tell, hasn't invited anyone out in all that time.'

'He might have a complete social circle *outside* the hospital,' Helen suggested reasonably. 'It would probably get pretty claustrophobic if your entire life was spent with the same set of people.'

'But that's exactly what he does,' Annie declared. 'He even lives in one of those tiny rabbit hutches they call staff accommodation, so he's never more than five minutes away from the job.'

Before Helen had time to absorb the startling infor-mation the lab results arrived and there was a phone call from MRI with an update on the waiting time until they could safely send the next patient across.

It wasn't until she'd returned home at the end of her shift and was towelling herself dry after a quick shower that she remembered what Annie had said. Suddenly she found herself wondering just what sort of man she was working for.

For all that Annie had said that he hadn't been known to go out in the three years that he'd been at St Augustine's, Noah certainly wasn't antisocial. In fact, Helen had noticed that he made a point of being available for the parents of his young charges whenever they needed to talk to him, as well as spending endless hours in the operating theatre and on the ward.

It had just never occurred to her to wonder where he lived that he was able to appear so rapidly when he was paged—certainly she had never thought that a man of his age and seniority would be resident at the hospital.

'I must have been going around with my eyes shut the last couple of months,' she muttered as she wielded the hairdryer on her shoulder-length hair, pulling a wry face at the nondescript mousy shade it was these days as she wound it expertly into a twist and clipped it out of the way.

She hated her hair looking like this, and longed for the long blonde tresses which used to tumble halfway down her back but. . . She shrugged, her eyes seeking out the faint scars that marked the surgery she'd had to undergo after the crash, at once grateful and sad that the face looking at her was only barely recognisable.

Her surgeon had wanted to do one final operation, believing that he could improve on his initial restoration of her shattered cheek-bone, but by that stage she'd had enough. Her face still bore an intriguing degree of asymmetry, but the work he'd done should be sufficient to help her achieve her ultimate goal.

For now, she was stuck with what she'd got—there were more important things on her mind. Perhaps, one day. . .

She pulled her thoughts up sharply.

*If* that day ever came it would mean that a miracle had occurred—and the last she'd heard, miracles were in rather short supply. She'd do far better to set her sights on the more immediate future, and for that she had to make a decision about what she was going to wear for the meeting tonight.

Her palms were damp with a combination of excitement and apprehension as she smoothed them down the sides of her silky trousers before she reached out to press one trembling finger to the bell.

She hadn't realised until the taxi drew up outside the entrance that she'd been brought to a private house. The

address Noah had given her had included a house name
rather than a number, so that she'd expected the venue for
her first meeting with the team to be a quiet restaurant.

Suddenly she was beset by the fear that she was going
to appear hopelessly over-dressed in the wrap-over cream
silk evening blouse and deeply pleated trousers, and she'd
actually taken a step backwards in the hope of disappearing
from view before anyone saw her when the door opened
and she was trapped.

'Hello, gorgeous!' drawled an appreciative male voice
with an obvious Irish lilt. 'Please, darlin', make my day
and tell me that you're Helen Morrisey!'

He reached out and grasped her by the elbow, as if he
was afraid she was going to disappear, and she found
herself looking into teasing green eyes surrounded by more
freckles than she'd ever seen before and topped by deep
auburn curls.

'I'm Helen Morrisey,' she confirmed with an answering
smile and allowed herself to be drawn into the vestibule,
suddenly knowing that everything was going to be all right.

'Can I take your clothes off?' he enquired helpfully,
and grinned widely when she gasped and whirled to face
him with shock in her eyes until she met the devilry in
his and allowed herself to relax enough to reply.

'You can take my wrap but, as we haven't even
exchanged names, I think anything else would be rather
premature,' she replied archly, astounded to hear herself
sounding so at ease. She'd never had much chance to
practise such banter and couldn't understand where the
words had come from.

'Noah!' he called over his shoulder. 'Come quickly and
introduce me to this gorgeous woman so she'll take her
clothes off for me!'

'Peter. . .!' His deep voice preceded him as Noah Kincaid came to the doorway, the reproving tone belied by the quirk at the corner of his mouth. 'Behave yourself, or she'll bail out before we've got her properly hooked.'

'Sorry, boss man,' Peter apologised with a mock tug at his wildly curly forelock. 'I'll behave myself, sure I will.'

'For all of thirty seconds, going on past performance,' Noah chided. 'Helen.' He turned to face her fully and she was stunningly aware of the impact of his deep blue eyes, their expression strangely shuttered as they met hers for the first time that evening.

'This reprobate is Peter Keenan, and he's our anaesthetist,' he said with an unconsciously graceful gesture of one hand. 'Pete, as you've probably realised, this is Helen Morrisey—our new theatre sister.'

Helen was barely aware of Peter's engaging chatter, her whole attention riveted on the casual elegance of Noah's long lean body as he led the way into a double-aspected lounge-diner.

She was hardly aware of her surroundings as her eyes took in the slim hips and long legs simply clad in stone-coloured chinos, appreciating the way the stark black of his shirt highlighted the sun-bleached streaks in his dark blond hair.

He turned and gestured to the two of them to make themselves comfortable and she found herself watching his every move, unable to drag her eyes away as he poured each of them a drink before stationing himself in front of a wide expanse of glass looking out onto a secluded garden.

The light behind him silhouetted the proud carriage of his head and the width of his shoulders but, although she was only too aware that the fading light was falling directly onto her own face, she was no longer able to see him so clearly and at last the strange spell was broken.

'. . .made you volunteer to sign on with Captain Bligh?' Peter was saying, and Helen suddenly realised that the words had been directed at her.

'Oh. . .er. . .I enjoy travel, and. . .' Lord, what *had* she written in her application, she thought as she frantically cast about for inspiration, her hand slippery on the tall glass of orange juice she'd asked for.

'How good is your Arabic?' Noah demanded suddenly.

'Oh, come on, Noah!' Peter objected. 'What would a pretty woman like Helen be doing learning. . .?'

'Not perfect,' Helen replied, ignoring Peter's interruption. 'I would have difficulty understanding a discussion about high finance or nuclear physics but, as far as everyday conversation goes, I'm pretty fluent.'

'What about medical terminology?' he challenged.

'I've been working on it,' she said, lifting her chin a notch as she felt the heat wash over her cheek-bones.

'Good God! Do you mean it?' Peter broke in, his voice full of amazement. 'You've actually been learning Arabic?'

Helen smiled distractedly in his direction, without looking away from Noah's still form—almost as if she was afraid to take her eyes off him.

'Why Arabic?' Noah's probing question still held an air of challenge.

'I began my training in London and, as with all of the hospitals in the capital, we saw patients of many different nationalities,' she began, relaxing a little now that she was only having to supply simple facts. 'I could see how hard it was for the ones who couldn't easily communicate with the medical staff; how much more frightening it was for them not to be able to ask even the simplest of questions. . .'

She detailed the days of terror endured by one patient who hadn't realised that every tumour diagnosed wasn't necessarily malignant.

'Anyway,' she continued, 'after I joined a group of nursing colleagues on a holiday in Tunisia and found that, with a bit of practice, I could actually make myself understood I decided it was something I would have a go at. . .' And, she thought to herself, it was something that she'd bitterly regretted when it had resulted in her meeting Mahmoud. . .

'Well, it will certainly come in useful for us,' Noah said quietly, overriding Peter's further exclamations of admiration. 'We usually end up working with the regular staff in the hospitals where we visit and, although the majority of them seem to speak English as a second language where medicine is concerned, it's always so much easier to deal with the patient's relatives in their own tongue.'

'I take it you have quite a number of patients of Arabic origin. Do most of them travel to England for treatment?' She found herself holding her breath as she waited for his reply, forcing her free hand to lie quietly in her lap when she really wanted to cross her fingers.

'That depends largely on their circumstances and which country they come from,' he explained. 'Some patients have very complex problems which their own hospitals haven't the trained staff to deal with.

'Sometimes their own government will pay for them to come to England for treatment, but others who aren't fit to travel—or those who have wealthy parents or patrons who are willing to fly a surgeon out to them—can be treated in their own country.'

'I can imagine that could be a bit like walking a tight-rope, as far as the local medical facilities are concerned,' Helen commented. 'Do they ever object to strangers coming in and telling them what to do?'

'Sometimes,' he admitted with wry understatement, and when Peter snorted he threw a telling glance at his colleague.

'It seems as though diplomacy and tact come before surgical skills while we're building up a rapport with the local team,' Peter confirmed, with the first serious expression Helen had seen on his face.

'Each time we have to remind ourselves that, no matter how frustrating it is, we're going to be working with them during the run-up to the operation and they'll be assisting us in Theatre and we know we'll be leaving the majority of the patient's recuperation in their hands.'

'I suppose, in spite of the fact that it's the patient who's most important, some of them could see your presence as a slight on their own skills. So, if you get off on the wrong foot. . .' Helen pulled a wry face, knowing that she didn't need to finish the sentence.

'*Our*,' prompted Noah and, when Helen turned a puzzled gaze on him, he explained. 'You said, "your presence" when you should have said "our presence",' he clarified. 'You're part of the team now, for better or worse.'

'You make it sound like a marriage,' Peter said with a laugh, but there was no answering smile from Noah.

'When a team works well together it *should* be like the ideal marriage,' he said, the slight edge to his voice catching Helen's attention. 'Each member has to pull together and work for the good of the whole, rather than one person dominating and the other blindly following—or both pulling in opposite directions.'

Helen smiled sadly to herself, recognising the idealism she had once shared, and she wondered what events in his past had made Noah realise how rare such harmony was.

If only every marriage *was* like that, she thought wistfully, but she knew to her cost that it wasn't always possible. Her own brief attempt certainly hadn't achieved the rosy-tinted standards he was talking about. . .

The sharp peal of the doorbell broke the sudden silence in the room and Peter leapt to his feet.

'That'll be Soapy—late as usual,' he quipped as he leapt to his feet and bounded out of the room like an over-eager puppy.

Silence fell again, and Helen found herself dismissing Peter's apparent slip of the tongue as she began frantically casting about in her mind for something to say—anything, so that she wasn't aware of the fact that Noah's eyes had hardly left her since he'd stationed himself in front of the window.

'Is. . .is he always like that?' she began hesitantly, then hurried on desperately, 'Doesn't it get exhausting after a while?'

Noah chuckled as he settled one hip on the wide window-sill, a deep enticing sound which gave the strange impression of wrapping itself around her.

'It would—very quickly—when we have to spend so much time together, but I promise you he'll settle down to being only mildly manic as soon as he gets to know you. It's just a symptom of his shyness.'

'Shyness?' Helen nearly choked on a sip of orange juice. 'He's the last person I'd suspect of suffering from that!'

'As with most people, he's learned to hide behind a form of camouflage,' Noah said quietly, the words striking an instantly responsive chord in Helen. She knew about hiding her thoughts and feelings only too well. . .

The evening light was fading fast but there was just enough falling over him—now that he had turned partially towards her—to finally allow Helen a glimpse of his expression, and she was startled by the depth of sorrow she could see behind the mask of calmness he wore.

She knew from working with him that he was always very self-contained and reserved, but had always believed that this was partly the result of the weight of responsibility that rested on his shoulders day after day. This was the first time that she had been forced to realise that he, too, might be hiding secrets behind protective camouflage.

She was quite shocked to realise that she found the idea more than a little intriguing, and hurriedly turned her gaze to the refined good taste of the room.

'This is a lovely house—so peaceful, in spite of being so close to the centre of town,' she commented, suddenly wondering who it belonged to.

'It's mine,' he confirmed, almost as if he'd read her mind. 'We. . .I lived here when I was married, but after my wife died. . .' He shrugged. 'I decided it was more convenient to be on the spot at the hospital.'

'Died?' Helen questioned in a shocked whisper, totally ignoring the rest of his words. 'Oh, God. I'm sorry.'

'An aortic aneurysm,' he said succinctly, using the term for the bulge in the damaged wall of one of the main vessels around the heart.

'How ironic.' Her voice was sad as she contemplated the fact that his wife had died of a condition which was part of his specialty. 'I take it you had no idea?'

'None,' he confirmed shortly. 'But *she* did—that's why she married me.'

'What. . .' Helen gasped in disbelief.

'Yes,' he confirmed with a wintry smile. 'She'd been warned that her condition meant that she might never be able to have a child, but that just made her more determined to try. So she picked a heart surgeon for a husband, in the mistaken belief that I'd be able to work the miracle her own doctor couldn't.'

'But. . .' Helen tried to interrupt, her senses bombarded by the confusing mixture of Noah's crisply unemotional words and the pain she could see in his eyes.

'Unfortunately,' he continued inexorably, 'she hadn't found a way of breaking the news to me—either of her heart condition or her pregnancy—before the combination killed her.'

'Oh, Noah. I'm so sorry,' she whispered, her voice full of anguish for his double loss.

'So was I—for the innocent child who never got a chance to live because of her selfishness.' His face took on the shuttered expression she'd seen before, but now she realised what was hidden behind it.

'Right, me darlin's,' Peter began, with all the aplomb of a sideshow barker as he entered the room again. 'Listen up while I make all the introductions.'

'Oh, Pete! Put a sock in it!' The amusement was clear in the softly husky tones of the young woman he was ushering into the room. 'We can manage perfectly well without a fanfare.'

'But, Soapy. . .' he remonstrated, sounding just like a little boy denied the last biscuit in the packet.

'. . .and that's *another* reason why I can put up with morning sickness with equanimity.' She turned on the hapless anaesthetist with both fists planted firmly on her hips. 'Every time I make a minute inspection of the cleanliness of the floor behind my toilet I tell myself that the discomforts of pregnancy are all worth it just so that I don't have to suffer being called ''Soapy'' ever again!'

'But, Soap. . .er. . . Sophie,' he corrected himself hastily when she made a threatening pass with one set of knuckles, just missing his nose.

Noah burst out laughing and straightened up from the window-sill to do his duty as referee.

'Enough, you two!' he ordered. 'What sort of impression are you making on Helen?'

'Don't mind me.' Helen waved a dismissive hand. 'After all, you invited me here to pick Sophie's brains and already I'm learning at first hand how to deal with Peter.'

'Hey! Not fair!' Peter protested over the combined laughter of the other three.

'Don't worry, Pete,' Sophie consoled him with a pat on his cheek and a wicked grin in Helen's direction. 'You'll get your chance to impress her when she sees what a good anaesthetist you are.'

'Some consolation,' he grumbled as he flopped back into his chair. 'First she refused to take her clothes off for me, then you show her that a five-foot flea frightens me. . .'

'If you two have quite finished?' Noah didn't even need to raise his voice to have them all paying attention, and Helen was impressed by his effortless resumption of control. 'If you'd like to follow me through to the kitchen, everyone can help to carry the food out here and we can eat and talk at the same time.' He led the way out into the hallway, without bothering to confirm that they were all dutifully following in his wake.

While Helen and Sophie waited for Noah to load Peter

with his share of goodies they quietly introduced themselves, and Helen found herself regretting the fact that the other woman's pregnancy would soon be stopping them from working together. It was a long time since she had felt so comfortable with a new acquaintance and she had the feeling that they could have become good friends.

As it was, she could only be glad that the advent of the child which had already begun to thicken Sophie's waistline had given Helen the chance to join the team—just when she had begun to fear that she would be too late. . .

# CHAPTER TWO

'I'M IMPRESSED,' Helen said as she waved a fork over her laden plate. 'All your own work?' She speared another mouthful of chicken pie, the pastry so perfect that it almost melted in her mouth.

'All except the dessert,' Noah admitted, without taking his eyes from his own meal, and Helen was surprised to see a hint of colour darken his high cheek-bones.

'I've tried to persuade my husband to take up cooking, but without any success,' Sophie chimed in mournfully. 'Unfortunately, I was already married by the time I found out what a good cook Noah is, otherwise. . .' She glanced across at Helen with a cheeky grin.

'Do you do a lot of cooking?' Helen was fascinated all over again. This was a totally unexpected side of Noah's character.

'I find it very relaxing,' he explained, without a hint of apology in his tone. 'I can get all the aggression out of my system by chopping and kneading and then, when I've thoroughly unwound, I get to sit down to a tasty meal.'

'Beats take-away every time,' Peter admitted as he went back to the spread set out on a cloth-covered table for another large wedge of pie and a small mountain of the assorted side dishes. 'If I could cook like this you'd soon have to move me around on wheels.'

Helen chuckled as she tried to conjure up the mental image of his wiry frame bloated by gargantuan eating, and failed miserably.

'Don't kid yourself,' Noah butted in. 'You burn too many calories up in nervous energy to ever have a weight problem. You're the same, aren't you, Helen?' he challenged, turning towards her. 'I bet your weight doesn't change by much more than a couple of pounds either way all year.'

Helen felt the warmth rise up in her cheeks as she became aware of his clear blue eyes skimming approvingly over her slender figure, but the faint beginnings of pleasure were overshadowed by the memory of another appraising look—one which had made no secret of the fact that he was dissatisfied with what he saw.

'No,' she murmured softly, tamping down the nightmare visions of the enormous plates of food she had been expected to consume if she was to avoid another terrible scene. . .'It hardly seems to matter how much or how little I eat—I always end up the same weight.'

Almost against her will, her eyes were drawn across to mesh with Noah's watchful blue gaze, and she was suddenly afraid that somehow she'd given away too much. He was a keenly intelligent man, with more than his fair share of intuition, and she had a horrible feeling that at some future date he would come back to this topic again. All she could do was mentally keep her fingers crossed that she had the bad memories under better control next time. . .

'I didn't realise you'd applied for the job on Mr Kincaid's team,' Anne Denton reproached Helen the next day. 'I thought you were a ward sister.'

'I worked in Intensive Care and Theatre, as well as a stint on a ward in my last hospital,' Helen confirmed, without any hint as to how deliberate each move had been.

'When I applied here the post of ward sister was open, but I was hoping to be able to move across to Mr Kincaid's team when there was a vacancy.'

'Well, it's stood you in good stead as far as landing the job on the team is concerned,' her colleague said with admiration in her voice. 'From what I understand, you'll need to wear each of those hats in turn when you travel to some of the hospitals.'

'So I've been told.' Helen laughed wryly when she remembered some of the horror stories Peter had regaled her with last night.

'I expect your time with us is going to seem pretty tame once you start to swan off around the world,' Anne teased her. 'Do you know when you're going on your first trip? How much notice will you get?'

'There's nothing on the cards for several weeks, but how could you possibly think that coping with a ward full of children is *tame*?' Helen retorted with raised eyebrows. 'Coping with one or two on a part-time basis will probably have me resorting to crochet or cross-stitch to relieve the boredom.'

Anne leant towards Helen with a slight frown on her face and whispered conspiratorially, 'Are you an alien from outer space with no real human blood in your veins?'

'What?' Helen blinked.

'Well, no red-blooded woman would admit to boredom in the company of Noah Kincaid—it's positively inhuman!'

'Idiot!' Helen aimed a mock blow at Anne's shoulder. 'You ought to know as well as I do that even the pleasant-est companion can grow tedious if you're forced into each other's company for long periods.'

'In that case, perhaps you should think about what you

can do to change his status to something other than ''companion'', if you're afraid he might bore you,' Anne quipped saucily as she turned smartly in the direction of the ward to answer the call button which had just been pressed. . .and nearly collided with the man himself.

'Oops!'

Helen heard her young colleague gulp, and she could see the fiery blush spreading up the back of her neck as she dodged around his broad-shouldered figure and scurried away.

Not knowing exactly how much of the silly conversation he'd overheard, she found herself holding her breath while she waited for him to break the ghastly silence.

'Problems?' Noah Kincaid enquired coolly as he folded his arms and leant back against the doorframe, as though he had all the time in the world. 'Do I take it that staff nurse was giving you helpful advice about your love-life?'

Helen felt her own face turn to flame under his unexpectedly chilly blue gaze.

'Certainly not,' she objected, knowing that she was only telling half of the truth, and desperately hoping that he didn't challenge her for the real topic of conversation.

'Good,' he murmured in a silky voice. 'It can make things very difficult for the team if one of us has a troubled private life. . .'

'Well, you need have no fear of that in *my* case,' she declared staunchly, keen to dispel any last-minute qualms he might be having about her place on the team. 'I don't *have* a love life.'

It wasn't until she saw his dark blond eyebrows shoot up towards his hairline that she suddenly realised what she'd said. Inwardly she cringed and wished that the ground would open up and swallow her, but she knew there was no way she could recall the embarrassing words as she made herself stand mute under his silent scrutiny.

In the end, he just gave a single thoughtful nod, shouldered his way upright and turned the conversation towards the real reason for his presence on the ward.

'How has Mia been today? Mrs Lomax didn't seem very forthcoming when I stopped to speak to her.'

'Mrs Lomax was a bit tearful earlier, and I think she's still embarrassed about sounding off at me,' Helen said with a forgiving smile.

'It doesn't seem to matter how well their babies are doing—it's never fast enough,' he commented wryly. 'I told her that the scan results were excellent—the graft is doing its job perfectly.'

Helen was finally able to relax while he reviewed the status of each of the patients in her care, answering her queries and giving fresh directions in his usual concise manner.

Noah finished by briefing her on a young patient with a congenital cardiac defect, due to be transferred from another hospital the following morning.

'Give the parents a couple of hours to catch their breath while you get young Oliver's blood tests started, then he'll need ECG, ultrasound and X-rays with a contrast medium to show up the great vessels.'

'He's another TGA, is he?' Helen enquired, using the shorthand for the transposition of the great arteries of the heart.

'Yes,' he confirmed. 'And I'm hoping the tests tomorrow will show that the case is as straightforward as the initial information suggests. I need to check up on the size and position of the defect between the two sides of the heart but, all other things being equal, I'm hoping to be able to do a total correction in one go.'

He had finished initialling the various sets of paperwork, and was on his way out of her little office when he paused in the doorway and looked back at her.

'Why not?' he asked out of the blue.

'Pardon?' Helen looked up from the notes she had just clipped into Oliver Keogh's new file. She had the feeling that she'd lost the thread of the conversation. 'I don't quite follow. . .'

'*Why* don't you have a love-life?' he elaborated quietly. 'It can't be for lack of opportunity.'

Shock made Helen draw in a sharp breath, and old insecurities put an edge on her tongue.

'Am I supposed to thank you for the compliment?' she eventually said through clenched teeth.

'Not necessarily,' he returned calmly, apparently unaffected by her sourness. 'I understand there are some who view such old-fashioned habits as paying a woman a compliment in a rather unfavourable light. Nevertheless,' he continued, forestalling her attempt at interrupting him with a raised hand, 'I would still like to know the answer to my original question.'

'Why?' she demanded baldly, as her chin inched up at a challenging angle. 'What difference does it make?'

'Personally, absolutely none,' he said dismissively. 'But I am rather concerned about the effect on the cohesion of the team if you are given to rabid feminist rantings at the drop of a hat.'

'You'll find I'm very appreciative of a door being held open for me, or a seat being offered—as are the majority of women in the country—so you needn't fear any ranting on my part.' She closed her mouth with a snap and glared at him.

'And my original question?' he persisted stubbornly.

Helen huffed out a sharp breath. He wasn't going to let her off the hook.

'Shall we just put the situation down to force of circumstance—or are you equally willing for me to grill you about your reputedly celibate status?'

One corner of his mouth lifted in a wintry excuse for a smile.

'I didn't know you were so interested or I'd have told you,' he taunted softly.

'But I'm not. . .' she denied automatically, and less than truthfully. In reality, she surprised herself by how keen she was to find out all she could about this enigmatic man.

'You'd hardly expect a man of my age *not* to have some sort of sexual history,' he continued, with a steely edge to his tone. 'But, then, what would a young woman like you know about the deceptions practised within a less than happy marriage?'

Helen felt the blood drain from her face, but even through the roar that filled her head she'd heard the sound of pain in his voice—the same pain which almost overwhelmed her every time she was reminded of that terrible time in her life.

Her eyes clung to his with all the tenacity of a drowning man on a rope as she slowly fought down the nausea, strangely strengthened by his quiet presence and his steady gaze.

The sudden bleeping of his pager made them both jump and Helen wrenched her eyes away from his, breathing a silent sigh of relief when he had to reach for the phone.

Her deliverance was complete when Noah had to leave the ward immediately. She took full advantage of the following lull to brew herself a large mug of tea to soothe her frazzled nerves.

She must have allowed her defences to grow weaker than she'd realised if a chance remark could bring her close to collapse. She'd believed that the year and a half she'd spent learning to control every expression—almost her every breath—would have stood her in good stead.

Was it time to shore up the ramparts that she hadn't realised were crumbling or, worse still, did Noah Kincaid possess some uncanny instinct for finding her weaknesses?

Whatever the answer was, she couldn't afford to allow anything to deflect her from her purpose. Nash's life might depend on her and if that meant that she had to wrap her defences even more tightly around her to keep all distractions at bay then so be it.

Helen's new determination carried her through the next few days without a hitch.

The news that she would be taking Sophie's place on the team had spread rapidly, and several of her nursing colleagues had called in the ward to congratulate her.

Helen was surprised by the degree of interest.

She hadn't been at the hospital very long. In fact, the main reason she'd applied for her present post was the knowledge that Noah Kincaid was to be Nash's surgeon.

The possibility that she might be able to secure the coveted position of theatre sister on Noah's surgical team had started off being a secondary consideration until she'd discovered that Nash would not be travelling to England after all.

Then the position on Noah Kincaird's team had become the driving motive of her life, ensuring that she spent her every waking hour focused on her goal. Her social activities were virtually non-existent.

She tried to dismiss all the attention her successful appointment had caused as a symptom of the notorious hospital grapevine, but it took Anne Denton's fine nose for gossip to put her straight.

'You're a popular member of St Augustine's staff,' she declared when Helen finally managed to get rid of the latest visitor.

'Don't talk rot, Annie,' Helen scoffed to cover up her embarrassment. 'I'm just an ordinary person who gets on with her job.'

'But you also do it well enough to get the plum job on Mr Sexy's team, and without getting anyone's back up with jealousy—either of the fact you got the job or that you'll be working so closely with him.'

'I reckon it's more a case of all these visitors coming up here to look me over to put their minds at rest that I'm no competition for them.'

'If that was the reason they'd leave here spitting nails when they find out how nice you are but, as it is, they've all gone out smiling—and full of our biscuits!'

She turned the empty tartan-patterned tin towards Helen to show her what she meant, then tipped it upside down over the bin and tapped it to dislodge the last couple of stale crumbs.

'I haven't done anything,' Helen objected, mentally replaying the conversation she'd just had with the latest of her opposite numbers. 'Tess seemed perfectly polite over the fact that she hadn't got the job.'

'I don't believe you can be so innocent!' Anne squeaked. 'Tess is the biggest gossip in the whole hospital. As my grandmother would say, '''er mouth's so big you can put both 'ands in and still wind wool''!'

'Annie!' Helen choked on the desire to roar with laughter at the mental image the phrase conjured up. 'It's all just a flash in the pan. By tomorrow someone else will be the hot topic of conversation.'

'I wouldn't count on it,' her young colleague warned. 'If it's something to do with Dr Dreamboat it'll always attract attention from any female of any age, as long as she's got a discernible pulse!'

'I think we need to come to some sort of agreement here, Annie,' Helen began decisively. 'I promise to keep the biscuit tin supplied, provided my office is a totally swoon-free zone.'

Anne burst into giggles. 'You're no fun at all!' she complained. 'But if it means that you'll stop my stomach from rumbling between meal breaks then you've got a deal!'

Helen sent her young colleague back to work and pondered briefly on the twists and turns her life had taken since she started her nursing training at eighteen years of age.

At the time she hadn't really known what she wanted to do, and it had been the careers advisor friend of her last foster-mother who'd suggested nursing.

'You're good with your hands and you never panic when one of the little ones hurts themselves,' her foster-mother had commented. 'In fact, you cope far better with their bloody noses and skinned knees than I do!'

'And good nurses will always be in demand—even if they aren't always paid what they deserve,' the careers advisor had added honestly.

It hadn't taken Helen many weeks to realise that she had found her ideal niche. Her enthusiasm for her almost accidental choice of career had carried her through the

depressing periods of exhaustion and sadness with the
promise of the recovery of the majority of her charges.

She had made the decision to specialise in the surgical
field fairly early on, but her switch towards paediatrics
had only come when she had returned to nursing a year
and a half ago and realised that it might represent Nash's
only chance. . .

Her eyes were drawn to the latest arrivals on the ward
and her heart thumped when she saw Noah, escorting a
young couple in the direction of her office.

'This is Sister Morrisey, Mr and Mrs O'Brien,' Noah
said by way of introduction as they arrived at the door.
'Is the interview-room free, Sister? We need to have a
conference about little Sean.'

Helen swiftly organised for a tray of coffee to be prepared while Noah ushered them into the small room set
aside for such meetings and completed the introductions.

'Sister will be part of our special team in the operating
theatre when Sean goes down for his surgery, and she'll
be in charge of monitoring his initial recovery.'

'Have you seen lots of these operations?' Mrs O'Brien
questioned in a shaky voice, directing her words at Helen
as her hands worried at a large white handkerchief. 'It just
seems such a terrible thing to have to do to a little baby —
to have to cut his chest open and. . .' Her lips began to
tremble too much to allow her to continue.

'And because nothing like it has ever happened to you
before it seems so much worse,' Helen said kindly, remembering her own torment when she had been in their shoes.
'I must admit that the first time I was involved with this
sort of surgery I was as shaky as you are but, after the first
couple of days of misery, the little boy recovered well.'

'And is he still well?' Mrs O'Brien grasped at the idea

feverishly, almost as if it would be an omen for her own son's prognosis.

'As far as I know,' Helen temporised honestly, mentally crossing her fingers that Nash *was* doing well, before she continued, 'He had a palliative shunt performed, just like Sean's will be, but he's probably just about the age to have his second operation to correct the defect totally.'

'You almost make it sound like a normal procedure— as if it's part of normal growing up,' commented a very white-faced Mr O'Brien.

'For Sean, it will be,' Noah interjected. 'If we don't do this anastomosis—this artificial connection between two of his arteries—he won't have enough oxygen in his arterial blood, and this will cause all sorts of other problems—even threaten his life. After we've done the operation, with your care and love, he'll grow bigger and stronger until he's ready for the second stage.'

'Do you always have to put them through two operations? It seems such a terrible thing. . .'

'Not always,' he admitted. 'In fact, these days—if at all possible—we like to do the total correction straight away. Unfortunately, in some cases the pulmonary arteries aren't quite big enough or there are other defects which complicate matters. Then we have to settle for a halfway house while we wait.'

Helen handed round the coffee and biscuits when Anne arrived with the tray, then watched quietly while Noah drew a series of simple diagrams to explain what was wrong with the way their son's heart was working and what the proposed operation would do for him.

She knew that he'd already explained everything to them when Sean's problem had been originally diagnosed, but it was important that they should have all the information they needed to cope with the situation.

She'd seen him use this method for every parent since she'd come to work on this ward, but she was still impressed by the clarity of his explanation and his patience with the many questions each set of terrified parents asked.

'So,' Mr O'Brien began, his colour slowly returning as he became immersed in the complexities of the situation, rather than the emotional aspects, 'when you eventually do the total correction the shunt you're doing now will be removed?'

'That's right,' Noah agreed. 'When the structural malformation has been corrected he won't need the shunt any more.'

'And that should be when he's two and a half or three?'

'If all goes as well, as we expect, that's usually about right,' Noah confirmed with a smile.

'So what happens next?'

'Tests,' Helen said simply, then laughed at the face Mrs O'Brien pulled.

'More tests? He's had so many. . .'

'Yes. Lots more of them. Lab tests, to check on his blood; chest X-rays and an electrocardiogram—the full panoply so nothing is left to chance.'

'How long will all that take? Do we. . .will we have to wait here while. . .?'

'If either or both of you can go with Sean to the various departments we'd be delighted. It will help him to remain calm if he's with familiar faces.'

'We can stay with him?' The mixture of disbelief and hope in Mrs O'Brien's voice brought a lump to Helen's throat.

'Of course you can,' she said gently. 'These days, hospital policy means that parents are not only *allowed* to be with their children as much as possible, we actively *encourage* it. Anything that helps the children to feel more secure will help to speed their recovery.'

'Apart from the fact that, if the parents are helping with the everyday chores of washing and feeding, it releases the nursing staff to do the actual nursing,' Noah added, with an almost cheeky smile as he flicked a brief glance at his watch.

'Oh, Doctor, I'm sorry we've kept you so long.' Mrs O'Brien hurried into speech, sounding quite flustered. 'I'm sure you must have so much else you should be doing.'

'Please forgive my rudeness, Mrs O'Brien,' Noah apologised ruefully. 'But, actually, I was just wondering how long it is until lunchtime—suddenly I'm starving!'

The tense atmosphere was broken by a round of laughter.

'That wouldn't be a bad idea for the two of you,' Helen suggested to the young couple. 'Why don't you go into the ward and reassure yourselves that Sean is safely settled, then you can make your way to the cafeteria and get something inside you.'

'Excellent idea,' Noah agreed. 'It might be a long time before you get your next cup of tea or coffee—unless you're brave enough to risk those awful machines!'

Helen ushered everyone out of the little room, pausing briefly to load their empty coffee-cups on the tray and carry it out with her. She would hate to show the next set of worried parents into the room and confront them with an array of dirty cups.

'When will you be free to take your lunch-break?' Noah's deep voice was so unexpected that Helen nearly dropped the tray. As it was, the china rattled alarmingly as she took the last couple of paces into the compact kitchenette.

'Really!' she muttered under her breath as she slid her precarious burden onto the drainer. 'Someone ought to tie a bell on him so we can hear him coming. . .'

'But who's brave enough to take on the task?' the same deep voice murmured right in her ear, and she shrieked.

'Will you *stop* doing that!' she snapped as she whirled to face him, her pulse galloping at double its normal rate. 'It's enough to give someone a heart attack!'

'Sorry!' He raised both hands to shoulder height, with his open palms towards her in an attitude of surrender. 'I thought you knew I was behind you.'

'Well, I didn't,' she replied snappily, and turned back towards her self-imposed task while she waited for her heartbeat and her flushed face to subside.

'You didn't say when you would be taking your break. Any chance of it being some time soon?'

Out of the corner of her eye Helen saw Noah reach across the work surface, but she was concentrating so hard on her reaction to his presence in the cramped space of the little room that he was reaching for the first of the cups she had set to drain before she realised what he intended.

'You can't do that!' she objected in shocked tones as she gazed at his long-fingered hands deftly drying the sturdy hospital-issue china.

'Obviously, I can,' he retorted, reaching up to set the first dry item in place on the shelf before he repeated the procedure with the next one. 'It's something everyone has to learn to do at some time—and I'm going to run out of things to dry if you don't get cracking!'

'But. . .' Helen still couldn't quite reconcile what she

was seeing with the persona of the illustrious surgeon.

'But nothing, woman. Get on with it before I starve to death!'

The rest of the task was completed in record time and without another word being spoken until the sink was wiped out and the cloths put to dry.

'Now, then. Time for food,' Noah said, rubbing his hands gleefully. 'I know it's only hospital fare, but it will keep the boiler stoked well enough to perform.'

'But I wasn't intending to go down. . .' Helen began, but her words were dismissed with all the subtlety of a Centurion tank.

'If you're going to be my theatre sister this afternoon you need to get some sustenance inside you. No argument!' he continued when it looked as if she was going to interrupt. 'Tell whoever it is who has to know that you're leaving and let's go!'

Helen felt almost like a reluctant child being dragged to the dentist as she followed in his wake.

He left her no time to manufacture reasons to delay, the hand-over to Anne Denton being achieved with such speed that her sensibly shod feet hardly touched the ground before they were on their way again, travelling at warp speed down the corridor.

'I know the next couple of weeks are going to be a bit chaotic while you're juggling your various hats, but the ward *will* cope without you when you start accompanying the team abroad,' he pronounced over his shoulder. 'We're none of us indispensable.'

'I never claimed to be,' Helen retorted breathlessly, stung into defending herself by his apparently poor opinion of her. 'At the moment my theatre work is intermittent and my replacement on the ward hasn't arrived yet. Anyway, I never have been a clock-watcher, like some are—always waiting to disappear on the dot. . . And I've never left my ward without making sure that the senior member of staff on duty knows where to find me, if necessary.'

She collapsed gratefully against the wall of the lift as he pressed the button, then glared defiantly at him across its width when he settled himself against the opposite wall.

'I've also seen you stay on for hours of extra duty when one of your favourite patients needed you, and you've never begrudged a minute of it—that sort of dedication is partly the reason why I wanted you for the team. But—' his dark eyes fixed firmly on hers to stress his quiet words—'you won't do anyone any good if you let yourself get over-tired, or if you don't feed yourself properly.'

'Yes, sir!' she muttered under her breath as the lift doors opened at their floor, but she wasn't brave enough to chance a salute—he was the consultant, after all. . .

'You don't have to be quite so formal,' he murmured mockingly as he paced silently beside her towards the aroma of over-cooked cabbage, and she flushed hotly when she realised that he had heard her sarcastic retort.

She was silent while they waited their turn in the queue, pondering her unaccustomed sharpness towards him, until finally they unloaded their choice onto an empty table on the far side of the starkly functional room.

'I'm sorry,' she murmured penitently as soon as she was sure that she couldn't be overheard. She was usually so even-tempered that she'd never had to find words like this before. 'I shouldn't have been. . .shouldn't have said. . .'

'Oh, don't spoil it,' he broke in over her scrambled apology, a positively wicked expression in his eyes. 'I was looking forward to having you squirm.'

'Squirm? Ha!' Helen exclaimed indignantly, her spine stiffening again. 'I was only being polite. . .!'

Aghast at the words she heard issuing from her mouth, she pressed her lips tightly together—her eyes widening as she suddenly realised that she was doing it again. What was it about this man that took the brakes off her tongue?

It was that fugitive gleam in his dark blue eyes and the suspicion of a grin at the corners of his mouth that told her he was enjoying every minute of her discomfort, and she wadded up the paper serviette in her hand and threatened to throw it.

'Uh-uh!' he murmured with a shake of his head. 'If you want to maintain your usual low profile that's not a good idea, with the number of eyes likely to be watching!'

Helen subsided with a final fierce look and concentrated on her meal, only realising just how hungry she was once she tasted the food.

There was a more companionable silence by the time they finished eating, Noah fetching a second cup of coffee for each of them before he took a slim diary out of his pocket.

'I've had notification that there's been a change in plans when the team travels to Q'ran next month,' he began conversationally.

Just the mention of the country was enough to drain every vestige of colour from her face, but her sudden fear that Nash's operation might have been cancelled had her swaying in her chair.

'Helen?'

The tone of his voice only penetrated her paralysis when he laid one hand over her tightly clenched fist.

'I'm sorry. . .' She drew in a shuddering breath, her voice trapped in her throat as she finally focused on him. She had no idea how long he had been trying to regain her attention but there was open concern etched on his face.

'What happened?' he demanded quietly, his dark blond brows drawn together into a slight frown as he brought his keen intelligence to bear on her. 'What's wrong?'

'N-nothing,' she denied shakily, sliding her hand away from the distracting contact with his long lean fingers. She covered it with her other hand and cradled it out of sight in her lap, but she still found herself missing his warmth.

'Have they cancelled the visit?' she demanded, knowing the frantic pounding of her heart was making her voice quaver but powerless to do anything about it.

'No—far from it. They've actually asked if we can add a second child with the same problem. . .' His voice died away as he concentrated on her clammy face. 'Helen, what on earth's the matter? You've gone quite white.'

'I. . .I suppose I was surprised how soon we'll be going abroad. I hadn't realised it was less than a month. . .' As she concentrated on placing her cutlery side by side on her empty plate she knew that it sounded weak, but she wasn't in any fit state to think clearly—not when she was just recovering from the fear that all her plans had come to nothing.

There was a moment's silence, but she didn't dare look up as she felt his intense gaze on her face.

'Well, I hope you're up to date on all your jabs and that your passport is current,' he reminded her as he finally looked away to fish in his jacket pocket and then noted something in the diary with a slim pencil.

This time she couldn't help the shocked gasp which escaped her as she suddenly realised that she had completely overlooked the one most vital element in her plan—without a passport she couldn't travel to Q'ran to see Nash, but with a passport she doubted that the Q'rani authorities would ever let her into the country.

# CHAPTER THREE

NOAH had taken one look at her face and, without a word, had hustled her out of her seat and across the room almost before she'd had time to draw breath.

They were shut in the lift and he had pressed the button to set it going by the time she found her voice.

'I haven't finished my break yet,' she remonstrated quietly, knowing that she needed more time to sort her head out before she went back on duty.

'I know,' he growled. 'Out you get.' He stabbed his finger on the button to hold the doors open while he ushered her towards their destination with a firm hand at the small of her back.

'But I need. . .' She paused as she glanced around, realising that she wasn't on the right floor. 'We've come to the wrong ward,' she pointed out.

'No, we haven't. I'm taking you to my office.'

'But. . .'

'For heaven's sake, woman, will you stop arguing?' he broke in as he pushed a gleaming white-painted door open and hurried her inside. 'You look like a ghost, you're trembling from head to foot and you're *still* shouting the odds!'

Before Helen could draw breath he'd placed both hands on her shoulders and pressed her down into the bland grey upholstery of the chair closest to the door.

Relieved of the necessity of concentrating on locking her shaking knees to keep herself upright, Helen

47

slumped back against the welcome support.

'Right, now,' Noah began briskly, his dark blue eyes uncompromisingly intent. 'Don't you think it's time you told me what's going on here?' He swung a second chair round to face her, perching himself right on the front edge so that he almost seemed to hover over her.

'I don't know what you mean. . .' Cowardice prompted the lie and shame accompanied it with a flash-flood of heat in her cheeks as she watched him silently shake his head.

'Try again,' he prompted. 'But bear in mind that I won't be letting you out of this room until you tell me what I want to know.'

Her heart dropped into her sensible shoes with a sickening thud, but she hadn't got this far without developing a fighting spirit.

'You have no right to keep me here,' she declared swiftly, her chin tilted at a belligerent angle. 'And we're due in Theatre this afternoon.'

'You're quite right,' he agreed, and the hairs stood up on the back of her neck at the almost menacing tone of his quietly controlled voice. 'But remember that I will *not* put my team or my patients at risk so *unless* I find out what I need to know you won't be in surgery this afternoon, nor will you be accompanying us when we leave for Q'ran.'

Helen felt the angry colour drain away once again and her shoulders slumped in defeat. She could have coped with any other threat, but to put her trip to Q'ran at risk after all she'd gone through to get this far. . .

'All right,' she acquiesced dully, knowing that she had no choice. 'What do you want to know?'

There was silence for a moment and she almost felt as if she could hear him thinking.

'Well, for a start, I got the feeling that you were quite desperate to join the team.'

'You didn't have to give me the appointment if you didn't think I was up to it,' Helen pointed out defensively, forcing herself to meet his gaze with some semblance of calm even though she felt as though she were hanging over an abyss.

'No. I didn't have to give you the job but, then, you know as well as I do that your breadth of knowledge and your nursing skills are excellent, and you made it almost a foregone conclusion that you'd get it when you made certain to stress your knowledge of Arabic.'

Helen didn't comment because she knew that it was true. The careful research she'd done when she'd returned to nursing had determined her choice of posts, and no matter how tired she'd been at the end of her shift she had pushed herself to continue with her study of the Arabic language.

She'd realised that she would probably only get one chance to achieve her goal, and she wasn't going to fail through simple lack of effort.

'On top of that,' he continued inexorably, 'your reaction to the idea of losing the position tells me that the appointment to the team means a great deal more to you than just a job.'

He leant back in the chair, his elbows propped on the narrow arms and his fingers steepled so that he could tap his pursed lips thoughtfully while he continued to look at her.

'Also,' he murmured slowly, his eyebrows drawing together over the straight blade of his nose, 'I definitely get the feeling that you aren't particularly interested in the job for the travel possibilities. It's definitely this one trip—

the Q'rani trip—that matters to you. Now, how about telling me why?'

Helen's fingers were linked together, too, but in her case she was gripping so tightly that the bones of her knuckles showed white through the skin, almost luminous against the dark blue of her uniform.

Oh, he was clever! He'd noticed each small slip, each tiny reaction, and slowly but surely he had fitted them all together to make a picture—a devastatingly accurate picture.

'I've been there before,' she heard herself blurt out, the words almost erupting from her mouth with the pressure that had built up over the many days and weeks.

'And?' he prompted.

'There's someone there. . .someone I needed to see and. . .and this was the only way I could think of. . .' She swallowed heavily, forcing the lump down in her throat. To have come so close. . .

'Who?' he fired back instantly. 'A boyfriend? A lover? Don't tell me you're going through all this to try to rekindle a holiday romance?'

'No!' Helen shook her head in vehement denial. 'It's nothing like that. He's my son. . .!'

The anguish in her voice echoed round the spartan little room, but she was hardly aware of it as her eyes desperately observed the succession of expressions which crossed his face.

'You're married?' he queried in a curiously hollow voice.

'I thought I was,' she said bitterly, as her mind filled with the memories of the hasty trip to the register office before Mahmoud had whisked her away to Q'ran and an unfamiliar ceremony in an unknown language.

'I didn't realise that he already had a wife.'

Suddenly the tears which she had never allowed herself to shed rose up and overwhelmed her, her convulsive sobs interspersed with disjointed words and streaming tears— until a large white handkerchief was pressed in her hands and she was scooped up against a broad chest and rocked as tenderly as any baby.

'Shh, Helen, shh. You'll make yourself sick,' he murmured, as one hand cradled her head against his broad strength, and the other stroked her back in long sweeps from shoulder to hip and back again.

'I'm s-sorry,' she hiccuped and blew her nose yet again, the flood of tears hardly seeming to have diminished.

'There's no need to apologise,' he murmured in a husky voice which was infinitely soothing. 'It seems to me that this avalanche of emotion was long overdue.'

It was several minutes more before Helen finally got herself under control and lifted her head away from the comfortable warmth of the angle between his shoulder and neck, and realised for the first time that she was actually sitting on Noah's lap.

'Oh, God!' Her voice came out in a strangled moan as she frantically scrambled to her feet. He'd briefly tightened his arm around her shoulders, as though he wanted her to stay where she was, but embarrassment lent her strength.

'You'd better sit down while you catch your breath,' he advised calmly, and Helen found herself doing exactly as he suggested, slowly beginning to register what was going on around her.

One of the first things she realised was that Noah had apparently been completely unaffected by the fact that she'd been sitting on his lap, even though she was still painfully aware of every millimetre of bone and muscle which had supported her and held her.

She could even remember the deep regular beat of his heart and the way she'd been able to hear his soothing voice as a fascinating rumble through the wall of his chest.

She also noticed that the fine dark fabric of his beautifully tailored jacket now sported a large damp patch on one shoulder, and his once immaculately laundered handkerchief was damp and mangled beyond recognition.

'Do you think you're ready to begin at the beginning and get the whole thing off your chest?' he prompted. 'Perhaps it's time you did.'

'Time?' Helen repeated thoughtfully, wondering if he was right, then, 'Oh, God! What's the time?' she demanded in horror as she grabbed for the watch pinned to the front of her uniform, then leapt to her feet when she suddenly realised how much time had passed. 'I should be getting back to the ward. Sean O'Brien needs his premed if he's going to Theatre.'

'Sit still a minute.' Noah raised a calming hand towards her while he reached for the telephone with the other. 'I don't think you're in a fit state to go charging around the hospital yet, do you?'

Helen had to admit that she was feeling like the wrong end of a long wet week, and subsided again gratefully as she heard him speak to Anne Denton to advise her of Helen's whereabouts and confirm Sean's dosages.

'Now, then,' Noah's deep rumble drew her out of her mental meanderings. 'That's all organised, so tell me how it all started.'

Helen's mind went back to when, as a brand-new staff nurse, she had first met Mahmoud. . .

She'd felt uncomfortable at first when she'd noticed the way his eyes had followed her while she'd been taking care of his uncle Ahmad, who was over in England for cardiac bypass surgery.

It was only when the older man had been transferred out of Intensive Care that Mahmoud had begun openly courting her with expensive presents and expansive compliments.

For the first time in her life Helen had felt like Cinderella at the ball, and when she had shyly rebuffed his attempts at greater intimacy he had proposed.

'What did your family think? Didn't they warn you to take your time to get to know him?'

'There was no one to tell,' she said simply. 'I never had that sort of close relationship with any of my foster-families. There was only Lisa. . .'

She felt the tears welling up again, and blinked frantically to stop them spilling over.

Lisa had been the closest thing she'd ever had to a sister, in spite of the fact that they'd only met during their last year in care.

When she'd finally introduced Mahmoud to Lisa he'd been so charming that she'd been equally bowled over, and hadn't seen anything wrong with the fairy-tale speed of their wedding.

'So, what went wrong?' Noah's voice drew her back from the dark corners filled with shadowy regrets.

'What didn't?' Helen countered with a bitter laugh. 'Apart from the opulence of the honeymoon. . .' She paused to grimace then murmured quietly, almost as if she'd forgotten he was there, 'although even that wasn't worth remembering. . .'

'Helen. . .?'

'I'm sorry. . .' She shook her head, as though trying to

get rid of the clinging memories. 'I'm sure you don't really want to hear. . .'

'Tell me,' he interrupted firmly, 'all of it.'

Helen drew in a steadying breath and began again.

'I didn't find out until we returned to his home that he already had a wife, Fatima, but by then I was pretty sure that I was pregnant so. . .' She shrugged. 'I'd resigned from my job so I didn't have any money, and I had nowhere to go. Once I told Mahmoud about the baby I was pampered to within an inch of my life, so I believed him when he told me that he'd divorced Fatima. . .I suppose I *wanted* to believe it was true. . .'

'And when the baby arrived?' Noah prompted, his face carefully empty of expression.

'Nash,' Helen murmured and felt the smile creep over her face. 'He was so beautiful, right from the minute he was born.' Her voice caught on the words. 'That's why I couldn't believe it when the paediatrician told me there was something wrong with him. I insisted that I wanted a second opinion.'

She shuddered when she remembered the furore at the insult her insistence had heaped on the country's top specialist, but Nash had been her son and she hadn't cared whose toes she stepped on.

'Finally, Mahmoud allowed me to bring Nash over to England, and I brought him to you.'

'To me?' The shock of her final words brought him bolt upright in his chair, his dark eyes intent as they searched her face. 'But. . . You must be mistaken. I very rarely forget a face, especially the parents of my patients, and I've never seen you before.'

'Not like this you haven't,' she agreed. 'But I didn't look like this when we first met.'

'Explain,' he demanded imperiously, his forehead pleated with confusion as he continued to gaze at her.

'After you'd operated on Nash—and when he was nearly recovered enough to leave the hospital—I went to a lawyer and applied for an annulment of my marriage on the grounds that since it took place in England it was bigamous.'

'But your husband had told you that he was divorced. . .'

'He lied,' she said flatly, shame making the words taste bitter on her tongue. 'It wasn't until I began to learn Arabic that I found out that Fatima couldn't seem to get pregnant, and Mahmoud desperately needed to produce a son to persuade his uncle that he was the right person to become head of the family when he died.'

'So you persuaded him to allow you to bring your son. . . God!' he swore hoarsely as the significance suddenly struck him. 'Nash! It's Nashir, isn't it. . .? It's your son that we're due to operate on in Q'ran next month.'

Helen nodded, wrapping her arms tightly around herself as though that would stop her feeling as if she were falling apart.

Noah straightened effortlessly out of his seat and began to pace agitatedly back and forth in the limited area between his desk and the door like a caged animal. He suddenly stopped and whirled to face her, his dark jacket parted over his gleaming white shirt-front by the fists planted on his hips.

'But. . .I don't understand. If you brought him over here how did he end up in Q'ran again? Did you lose your case in the courts? Was your husband awarded custody?'

'No, Mahmoud didn't even bother contesting the case, either in person or by lawyer. He just sent two of his bodyguards after me and they k-kidnapped Nash.'

The sobs building up in her chest nearly strangled the words as she relived the terror.

'We were in Lisa's car—she'd had a child's seat put in so that Nash would be safe.' She drew in a shuddering breath. 'Thank God she did because it was probably the only thing that saved his life when they forced us off the road.'

She closed her eyes tightly as she endured the replay of the world tumbling over and over around her as the car had plunged sideways down a steep embankment. Her mind was so occupied with the terrible memories that she hardly registered Noah's horrified exclamation.

'Lisa was killed outright,' she whispered, looking up at him as the tears began again. 'She was only taking us from the hospital to the flat I'd found, but when they sideswiped the car she hit her head against the door pillar. The post-mortem showed that the shock of the impact shattered the top vertebra in her neck—I think they call it a hangman's fracture, don't they?'

'And you were hurt too,' Noah murmured with utter certainty as he came closer and crouched in front of her chair, his sharp eyes mapping her face as though he'd never seen it before. 'You had to have one side of your face rebuilt.' He traced the shape of her cheek-bone and around her eye-socket with gentle fingertips until he found the tracery of fine silvery lines, almost hidden in her hairline.

'I think that was what saved my life in the end.' Her voice was growing noticeably husky and she tried to tell herself that it was caused by the strain of all the talking and tears. It couldn't possibly have anything to do with the strange tingling which seemed to follow his touch.

She forced the renegade thoughts away and concentrated on putting that terrible scene into words.

'The way Lisa was hanging from her seat belt she was obviously dead, and I must have looked so horrendous— with my face all covered in blood—that they thought I was dead too and didn't bother to get close enough to make certain.'

'You can't mean that you think they *deliberately* tried to kill you?' Horror filled his voice as the meaning behind her words registered.

'I listened to them climbing down after the car to see what had happened to Nash, and I heard them talking to each other in Arabic.' Inside her head she could hear their voices all over again, and it was as if she was once more trapped by the buckled metal of the side of the car.

'One of them was afraid that they'd killed Nash, and said that Mahmoud would kill both of them if they had. The other one said that it was Mahmoud's fault—that he'd told them to do it because he couldn't afford to let me take Nash away from him. He'd got too much to lose if he didn't prove to his uncle that he was master in his own house.'

'Did you tell the police what you heard?'

'I didn't *dare* tell them,' she said simply. 'I was so scared that Mahmoud's two thugs would find out that I was still alive and come back to finish the job.'

'Are you absolutely certain that's what you heard? You'd had a terrible blow to your head and you must have been drifting in and out of consciousness. Could you have imagined it?'

'No.' She shook her head sadly. 'I couldn't possibly have imagined anything as horrible as that. Anyway, if it was all in my imagination how would you account for two people speaking Arabic as they took my son away?'

'You're quite right,' Noah agreed. 'He didn't just disappear.'

'I heard them talking as they took Nash out of his seat. He was whimpering and shocked and they were talking to him in between blaming each other for what happened. They were terrified someone would come along and see them taking the baby and make a report to the emergency services before they could get away with it.'

'But what about afterwards? It would have been easy enough for them to check up whether you'd survived.'

'Apart from Nash's safety, that was the only lucky thing that happened that whole horrible day. The press managed to switch the names around, and in their report it said that Lisa had survived the crash.'

'So,' he said thoughtfully as he straightened up again and gazed blankly towards the institution-beige wall while he processed the lastest information she'd given him. 'They must have thought they'd got away with it because even if Lisa went to the police she wouldn't have been able to understand what they were saying, and she'd have no claim on the child.'

'Exactly,' Helen agreed, amazed by how quickly he'd grasped the different elements. 'They must have held their breaths while they waited to see if any enquiries were made, but after two years. . .'

'And you've been waiting all this time to go to see your son? Couldn't you have contacted the British consulate or something?'

'No! I daren't give Mahmoud even a hint that I'm still alive or he would send them after me again.'

'But surely they've had plenty of time to check up on your name—you're back working as a nurse again.'

'But not under my own name,' Helen admitted quietly.

'I know it's not strictly legal, but I was too scared that I'd never get a chance to see him again.'

'And what *is* your real name?'

'Eleanor Norris. That's why I chose my present name— so that they would sound similar enough that I wouldn't forget to answer.'

'Ah!' Noah suddenly gave a sigh of satisfaction as another piece of the puzzle fell into place. 'I've just realised why you went a ghastly putty colour when I mentioned your passport.'

'I'd suddenly realised that I couldn't apply for one under my assumed name, and if I tried to enter Q'ran under my real name it might ring bells.'

'So,' Noah said briskly as he sat himself back in the chair, 'what are we going to do?'

Helen paused in surprise, immeasurably heartened by Noah's unexpected sharing of her problem.

'I don't know,' she admitted. 'I haven't really had time to think about it, and I'm being torn in so many directions at once that my brain doesn't seem to want to co-operate any more.' She dropped her head into her hands and speared her fingers through her hair while she drew in a shaky breath to calm herself down.

'I think I might have a possible solution,' Noah murmured hesitantly into the silence.

'What?' Helen pounced eagerly. 'What solution?'

'Hang on,' he cautioned with a raised finger. 'I only said it was a possibility, but first I need to ask a few more questions.'

'Ask away,' she invited. 'If I can tell you anything that will help. . .'

'Helen. . .' He sighed deeply, his eyes very dark as he captured her attention. 'You *do* realise that it might not be possible to find a solution in time for the trip to Q'ran, and if we can't sort your problems out we'll have to replace you with another theatre sister?'

'No!' she wailed, and covered her mouth with a shaky hand as she contemplated the failure of all her plans and hopes. 'Oh, please! I've got to see him! I've got to!'

'Think about it,' he said urgently, speaking over her renewed sobs. 'We're not going on a sightseeing holiday. We're members of a highly specialised surgical team, and we've got sick children waiting for us to operate on them.'

Helen heard the intensity in his voice and the reality of his words penetrated her misery.

'You're right.' She drew in a deep shuddering breath as she fought to regain control of herself. 'Nash's health is the most important thing, but. . . Oh, God! I need to know if he's being looked after properly. I need to know if he's happy!'

Noah reached across the gap between their chairs and took her hand in his, the lean length of his fingers warm and comforting as they wrapped around her own much smaller hand.

'I've already received a copy of his most recent medical records and they tell me he's doing as well as can be expected. But I promise that if we have to leave you behind I'll take the time to find out how he is, and I'll take photographs to bring back to you. I know it's not the same as seeing him and touching him yourself, but at least it would put your mind at rest to a certain extent.'

'Yes, but. . .' She bit her tongue, a flood of guilt filling her as she realised she hadn't told him the true extent of her intentions. She didn't dare take the risk that it would be the final straw that stopped him helping her.

'Now, then.' There was a new briskness in his voice

and she gratefully left her guilty thoughts to one side. 'I'd better get on with those questions I needed to ask.'

He took the slim diary out from the pocket inside his suit jacket and turned pages until he found what he was looking for, his pen poised over the blank space.

'The first question involves your marriage,' he began incisively. 'Was it properly annulled when you applied to the court, and what happened about the custody of Nash?'

'The annulment was sorted out before Mahmoud sent his thugs to snatch Nash, and the court awarded me full custody. At the time I went on record as saying that I had no objection to reasonable visitation—after all, Nash was his son. . .'

For several minutes Noah fired questions at her about her efforts to change her legal documentation, and she watched his familiar decisive writing cover a second page of the notebook as he jotted down the information.

'OK,' he said thoughtfully as he finished writing. 'We need to check what forms of identification you would have to produce to be issued with a new passport, and we need to know if you can have one in your current name without your previous name appearing on it.'

He looked up as his pen finished moving.

'Anything else you can think of? Only we've got to get moving on this because, with Easter coming up, it can take several weeks or more to get a passport through if the annual flood of applications from holidaymakers has started.'

Helen was filled with the slow-dawning warmth of renewed hope, and she could feel the beginnings of a smile lifting the corners of her mouth.

'I can't think of anything at all—my brain is completely scrambled,' she said apologetically. 'Would you mind very much if I left it all in your hands?'

'Well, having chosen you as the best applicant for the position on the team, I suppose it's up to me to make sure that I do everything I can so that you can actually travel with us!' He smiled wryly.

Helen was seized with the mad urge to drag him out of his seat and whirl him wildly around the room. She'd been so afraid that when he heard about the primary reason she'd applied to join the team, and the fact that it could cause a major problem on her first trip with them, he'd be forced to replace her.

If she was honest, she could hardly blame him if he'd decided to do exactly that because the overall good of the team was more important to him than the private concerns of one individual member, no matter how good she was at her job.

But this was totally unexpected! To have him volunteer his own time and effort to make the enquiries necessary to get the tangle sorted out made her look at him in a whole new light.

There was a new spring in her step when Helen finally made her way back to the ward, her face completely denuded of makeup by the copious quantities of cold water she'd used to take away the redness her tears had left around her eyes.

'You don't really need it,' Noah had said gallantly when she'd commented on the fact, and she'd felt again the almost physical reality of the touch of his eyes over her face. 'Your skin is beautifully soft and clear, and your eyes don't need any artificial emphasis. . .'

His words died away and as she noticed the darkening

colour over his cheek-bones she felt an answering heat rising in her own face.

What on earth was happening to her? she thought as she waited for the lift to stop at her floor. She'd never been one for indulging in crushes, even as a teenager, and since her apparently fairy-tale marriage had deteriorated into a nightmare she hadn't had any interest in men at all—even the admittedly gorgeous Noah Kincaid.

That all seemed to have changed in the last few days.

Ever since that embarrassing conversation when she'd mistakenly believed that Noah was propositioning her she hadn't been able to help herself reacting to him, and it was making her strangely nervous.

She'd once heard the expression 'like a long-tailed cat in a room full of rocking chairs' and she knew now exactly what it meant. Even when she was at home she couldn't seem to stop thinking about Noah, and there was a strange air of expectancy hovering over her. The only thing she didn't know was whether the coming events were going to be good or bad.

After her usual visit to each of her charges on her return to the unit Helen crossed her fingers and sent up a silent prayer as she sank gratefully into the chair behind her desk. She gazed into the distance for a moment while she got her galloping thoughts into order.

In less than an hour she would be accompanying Sean O'Brien and his parents to Theatre, and then there would be several hours of strict concentration while she did her best to anticipate Noah's needs during the actual operation.

She closed her eyes and concentrated for a moment. She knew that if she was to regain her mental balance she had to empty her mind of all thoughts of Nash and the see-saw of emotions attached to the possibility of seeing him again.

If she was going to be of any use to anyone—and especially to little Sean O'Brien—she would even have to block out the strange magnetism she seemed to be developing where Noah Kincaid was concerned.

It was Mr Kincaid the surgeon she would be working with this afternoon, she reminded herself sternly. Any thoughts of the enquiries he was putting in motion would have to wait until later.

# CHAPTER FOUR

THE familiar sounds of the operating theatre were almost reassuring as Helen settled into the job she knew so well.

As ever, the cares and worries of her own life were left outside as she donned her green smock and trousers and, as she entered the brightly lit room, automatically cast a critical eye over the supplies laid out, ready for the operation to begin.

'Everybody ready?' Noah's deep voice preceded him as he entered the room, his scrubbed and gloved hands held away from any possible contamination and the bright gleam of his hair concealed by the ugly disposable elasticated hat.

'Sean's just arrived,' Helen confirmed. 'We're ready as soon as you are.'

He nodded, and Helen shouldered the swing-door open to signal to the anaesthetist.

The administration of the anaesthetic was just one more in a bewildering array of nasty things that had happened to Sean in his short life, but within seconds his pained cry had become a sigh of submission as he lapsed into unconsciousness.

'See you later,' Helen heard his mother whisper as she bent over him for a last kiss before she and her equally scared-looking husband were led away to begin their long wait.

Sean's little body was swiftly transferred to the operating table, and within minutes the anaesthetist had performed the various connections to his monitoring equipment and all but the operating field was draped in familiar green.

'Beginning,' Noah intoned as he held out one gloved hand for Helen to deliver the scalpel which would make the initial incision into the sienna-coloured painted skin.

Her concentration was absolute as she followed each familiar stage of the operation, but somewhere at the back of her mind she was storing the images of Noah's fluid sureness as he opened the tiny chest and exposed the beating heart.

'Ready for bypass,' he indicated soon afterwards, and Helen marvelled again at the way the heart grew pale and still when the circulation of blood was taken over by the anaesthetist's machinery.

'Time,' Noah instructed as soon as he'd settled the operating microscopes to his satisfaction, and Helen saw the automatic reaction as everyone glanced up at the clock on the wall. They all knew that this was the most dangerous part of the operation because even the most perfect surgical technique was useless if it took so long that the heart muscles were damaged by prolonged oxygen deprivation.

If that happened, Sean could die without ever waking up from the operation.

'Ready with the graft,' Noah warned, and Helen reached for the length of imitation blood vessel crafted out of Gore-Tex, which he would attach between the subclavian and pulmonary arteries.

She watched as he painstakingly positioned each stitch, then breathed a sigh of relief as he tested the joins by releasing the clamps holding back the blood.

'Nice and pink,' he commented as the colour of the heart muscle darkened with the returned flow. 'And a spontaneous return of rhythm,' he completed with obvious delight in his voice as he straightened up and rotated his shoulders to relieve the tension.

'And no sign of a leak,' Helen added, her wide smile hidden by her mask.

'And everything doing well from my end,' the anaesthetist chipped in.

'Well, then,' Noah said in a satisfied tone as he bent forward again. 'Time to finish putting young Sean back together.'

'How's he doing so far?' Noah murmured through his disposable mask as he joined her beside Sean's bed in the paediatric intensive care unit.

'His colour's better already, in spite of the trauma of the operation—not nearly so cyanosed.'

Noah held out his hand for the clipboard with Sean's observations and nodded when he saw the careful rows of figures, confirming their message with his own swift examination.

'I'll go and have a quick word with his parents and tell them they can come in—just for a quick visit,' he murmured as he handed the charts back.

'Just long enough to put their minds at rest,' Helen said, knowing that he'd be able to see the smile in her eyes over the top of her mask. 'Then I'll try to persuade them to get some rest. I don't think either of them slept last night.'

It was a relief to be able to allow her own feelings to colour her words as she spoke to Noah. Now that she had told him about Nash he knew how completely she could empathise with the parents of their patients, having gone through the same agony of waiting herself.

The memory of that awful time, and the fact that she'd

had to go through it alone, brought back to her the realisation that she still didn't know whether she was going to
be able to see Nash or not.

She drew in a shuddering breath and was startled to
feel the weight of a masculine hand on her shoulder. She
looked up just as Noah squeezed gently.

'Chin up,' he whispered, almost as if he had followed
her train of thought. 'I'm hoping to get some answers in
the morning.' His eyes, too, seemed to be smiling at her
before he turned and went to give the good news to Sean's
waiting parents.


Helen didn't know which piece of news she wanted first
when she reported for the start of her shift the next day.

Little Sean had been recovering amazingly well by the
time she had finally left the day before, and she fully
expected the glowing report she received from his ecstatic
parents when they greeted her at the door of the intensive
care unit.

'We were so scared that he wouldn't survive the operation,' admitted Mrs O'Brien.

'Even though everyone told us that Mr Kincaid was the
best one to do it, Sean just seemed too small to live through
something so. . .brutal,' her husband added honestly.

'We've had them smaller and younger,' Helen reminded
them. 'Some babies have to be operated on almost as
they're born or their brain would be starved of oxygen
and die.'

'It doesn't bear thinking about,' the young woman shuddered. 'It was bad enough with Sean, but at least we had
time to come to terms with it a bit.'

'Well, he's certainly proved that he's a little fighter,

hasn't he? At this rate, he'll be carrying you home instead of the other way round!'

Helen left the pair of them with their arms around each other while she went to tackle a small mountain of forms, but she had hardly begun to make an impression on it when the phone rang right beside her.

'Sister Morrisey,' she said, keeping one finger on the pile in front of her so that she didn't lose her place.

'Good morning, Sister,' replied the deep tones of Noah Kincaid's distinctive voice, and Helen's stomach clenched in anticipation.

'Any news?' she blurted out without any preliminary small talk, trusting that he would understand her urgency. 'Am I going to be able to go?'

'I can't be absolutely certain because we need to have another talk.' His voice sounded rather reticent over the phone, and she wished that she could see his expression. 'Can you arrange to take an early lunch-break?' he continued, and Helen had to force herself to concentrate to make sense of his words.

'How early?' She glanced at her watch and then across at the duty roster.

'Twelve?'

She did some quick mental adjustments and sent up a silent apology to the poor staff nurse who would end up having to wait the longest, then agreed.

'Come straight up to my office,' he directed crisply. 'We aren't so likely to be disturbed there.'

After a few more sentences about young Sean's progress he broke the connection, leaving Helen staring into space—her brain whirling as she tried to anticipate the problems that still had to be sorted out before she would be able to travel safely to Q'ran—and Nash.

She gritted her teeth and straightened her shoulders as new determination lifted her chin. She wouldn't know about the hurdles still facing her until she saw Noah at twelve o'clock. One thing she *was* certain about was that—some way, some day—she was going to see her son and find out if he was well and happy, and if not... well, that was another decision entirely.

'Come in,' Noah's voice invited when Helen knocked on his door just two minutes after twelve. It had taken some persuasive talking but, as usual, she had made certain to leave the patients adequately covered by competent staff. The fact that she had almost had to sign her soul away to coax some changes in off-duty time was something she'd live with. There was no way that she could have faced waiting any longer for this important meeting.

'Sir?' she began hesitantly when he continued writing furiously, uncertain whether he had realised who had come in.

'I'm sorry.' He flicked her a quick glance and a dis-tracted smile, indicating the chair she'd sat in last time she was there. 'Can you give me another minute to finish this?'

Almost before she'd nodded he was concentrating again, his head bent so that all she could see was the gleaming thickness of the dark blond hair and the familiar black slashing lines of his handwriting as his pen sped over the page.

Quietly she settled herself to wait, taking a strange pleasure in being able to observe him while he was too busy to notice her looking.

How could she have been working with the man for six months and not noticed how good-looking he was? she marvelled as her new perspective gave her a perfect view

of the clean, sculptured lines of the bones of his face and
the broad, powerful shape of his body. For the first time
she admitted to herself that Annie had been quite right
when she'd called him the sexiest man on the hospital staff.

The strange thing was that she had never really noticed
him before, and now she could hardly think about him
without her whole system going into overload.

Perhaps it was something to do with the gratitude she
felt towards him for trying to sort out the mess she'd made
of her life. Or perhaps it was just an indication that, after
the living nightmare of her marriage, she was at last
returning to normality, and he was the first male to trigger
her long-dormant hormones.

'Right. Finished!' he announced as he capped the pen
and looked up at her, almost catching her gazing at his
long tanned fingers. Was she destined to go through her
life making a fool of herself in front of this man? 'Sorry
about that, but the paperwork follows you all the way up
the ladder.'

He pulled a wry face and leant back in his chair, groan-
ing as he stretched both hands over his head until his shirt
began to slide up out of the waistband of his trousers.
Helen dragged her eyes away with an effort.

'Have you managed to find any of the answers?' she
asked, determined to get her mind on the matter in hand.
'Is it going to be possible for me to go?'

'Yes, it's going to be possible,' he began, only to be
interrupted.

'Oh, God, thank you,' she moaned, and collapsed
against the upholstered back of the chair, close to tears as
relief flooded through her.

'But. . .' he added, raising his voice over her interruption, and her heart sank again.

'But what?' she demanded. 'You *said* it was possible.'

'But not necessarily safe—unless you're willing to take some extra precautions.'

'Precautions? What do you mean?' Helen slid forward on the seat and clasped her hands tensely on her lap. 'Surely you know by now that I'd do anything I have to if it means I can be with Nash.'

There was silence in the small room, and Helen could have sworn that she could hear her hair growing while she waited for Noah to speak.

Finally he seemed to come to a decision, and he stood up and came round to sit in the chair set at right angles to her own.

'I found out that it's a fairly simple matter to change your name to whatever you want. Apparently, you could even call yourself Mickey Mouse, if you were silly enough.'

'So?' She was too wound up even to attempt a smile.

'So, the problem comes when you want to use your new name for legal purposes—because you can't, without getting all sorts of signed declarations.'

'Couldn't I do that?'

'In the ordinary way that would be perfectly adequate but in your case, where you could be in danger if anyone knows your former name, it's no use at all because *both* names have to be on the document.'

'But that defeats the object,' Helen wailed despairingly. 'How can I get round that stipulation?'

'First of all, by going to a solicitor and having them draw up a statutory declaration of change of name.'

'What good would that do?' she objected. 'Wouldn't it just make it more obvious that I'd changed my name?'

'In the first instance, yes,' he agreed. 'But if you were

then to apply for a subsequent legal document, using the statutory declaration as proof of your new legal identity, the subsequent legal document would only contain your new name.'

'It sounds so complicated,' she murmured, and was surprised to see a flush of colour darken his face as he looked away from her. Sudden contrition struck her. He must think she was so ungrateful for all his efforts, to be complaining like this.

'So, what legal document *could* I apply for that wouldn't show my change of name?'

This time the silence lasted for several long heartbeats, and Helen felt a warning shiver run the length of her spine and raise all the hairs on the back of her neck.

'A marriage licence,' he said quietly, his sapphire eyes seeming to grow even darker as she gazed at him in utter shock.

'But. . .' She shook her head wordlessly, speechless with dismay. 'I'm not. . .I can't get *married*!' Her voice was uneven with shock, and rose shrilly at the sheer impossibility of the idea. 'I *can't*!'

'Not even if it means you'll be safe to go to see your son?' Noah prompted in a husky voice. His eyes dropped briefly from hers to fasten on his linked hands which hung between his knees, his elbows planted on tautly muscled thighs.

'I. . .' The words she had been about to speak froze in her throat as his eyes returned to hers, capturing her with the intensity of twin lasers.

'What about a marriage of convenience?' he suggested softly, then continued to pile shock on top of shock when he added, 'I'd be willing to lend you *my* name.'

Helen stared at him, beyond amazement.

'You. . .?' she gasped. 'But you don't want. . . We aren't even. . .' She stopped, unable to form a coherent sentence—unable to string two words together as her brain whirled uselessly. Finally, she found the only word which mattered. 'Why?'

Her bluntness seemed to amuse him because even his eyes smiled when his face creased into a strangely boyish grin.

'Why marriage, or why me?' he prompted gently.

'Well, both, I suppose,' she said, feeling strangely disconnected from the whole conversation—as if she would be waking up any minute to find it was all a dream.

'As I explained, the marriage certificate would help to hide the fact that you'd changed your name—very effectively, in fact, because you would be changing it a second time. That would mean that even in the unlikely event that someone in Q'ran decided to check up on you they'd be even more unlikely to think that you'd change it again by marriage.

'As for the "why me?",' he continued patiently, 'we'll be going on the trip together anyway, and I know the situation so it would make sense to have me there beside you to reinforce your new status.'

'But couldn't it be someone here in England? The authorities in Q'ran don't have to be able to see my husband. . .'

'Have you got another candidate willing to step in at a moment's notice?' He raised a quizzical eyebrow over darkly intelligent blue eyes.

Helen flushed and looked down at her short, unpainted nails. 'No,' she mumbled. 'No one.'

'So.' Noah straightened up with an air of satisfaction.

'Does that mean you want me to go ahead and make an appointment with my solicitor?'

'Now?' Her eyes flew up to meet his and she licked her lips nervously. Everything seemed to be moving too fast for her to come to terms with it.

'Well, you need to get the statutory declaration sorted out before anything else but, having said that, it doesn't make any sense to delay the marriage either. I would have thought it would be a good idea for everyone to get used to the idea before we set off for Q'ran.'

'Everyone?' she parroted, aghast. 'You're going to tell other people what we're doing?'

'Were you intending to keep it a secret?' he countered, apparently completely untroubled by the magnitude of what they were about to do. 'What good would secrecy do for your situation in Q'ran if it makes someone suspicious and they start checking up on you? In fact, if the rest of the team only found out that we were married when we declared the fact on arrival it would be even *more* likely to trigger off alarm bells!'

'But. . .'

'Of course, we wouldn't be telling them *everything*,' he added easily, totally ignoring her interruption. 'Just the fact that the two of us had decided to get married.'

'But. . .' Helen began again in a last-ditch attempt then subsided, knowing that she was wasting her breath. Ultimately she had to concede that there was perfect logic in his arguments, and her shoulders slumped as she nodded her silent agreement.

Where was the point in arguing when he was right?

'Are you on earlies tomorrow?' There was no hint of Noah's thoughts or feelings in his calm voice or in the efficient way he turned the pages as he consulted his diary again.

'I don't. . . No, I'm day off. . .I think. . .' Helen blew out an exasperated breath. 'My mind's in such a muddle that I can't even remember what day of the week it is!' She gazed at him, suddenly feeling very close to tears.

What on earth did she think she was doing? How could she calmly agree to marry a man who was little more than a stranger? Panic built up inside her and just as she drew breath to take back her agreement Noah distracted her by reaching out towards her.

'Here.' He offered the small oblong of paper he held and Helen numbly accepted it, at first hardly doing more than glancing in its direction.

A longer, second look confirmed the fleeting image seared on her brain.

'Is this. . .? this is Nash?' She could hardly bear to drag her eyes away from the small figure in the photograph long enough to see Noah's confirming nod.

'The photo was in the file sent over from Q'ran.'

'Oh, God.' She covered her mouth with one shaking hand as she tried to focus on the quivering image she held in the other. 'Oh, he's grown so much!' she whispered, awed by the unexpected chance to see her son like this. 'He was such a little boy when I last saw him—hardly more than a baby—but look how grown-up he is here. . .'

She glanced up at Noah, knowing that tears trembled on her lashes but unable to do anything about them.

'Can I. . .? May I keep it?' she pleaded huskily. 'I haven't got any others. . .'

'Of course you can.' His voice was a gentle caress over her raw nerves. 'Just remember to leave it at home when we set off for Q'ran—in case our luggage is searched.'

That reminder was enough to bring the reason for all the subterfuge home to her.

Suddenly her last-minute doubts seemed petty and foolish when a young, innocent child's safety and happiness were at stake. She would even contemplate marrying the devil himself if it meant being able to see Nash again, and Noah Kincaid was a long way from being satanic.

Helen looked at the man sitting opposite her for long silent moments while all the thoughts finally slotted into place.

She had been working with him and around him for the last six months, and knew that he was a hard-working, honourable man. The fact that he could make such a quixotic gesture as to offer his own name as protection so that she could see the child so cruelly snatched away from her was something that she couldn't have foreseen, but the more she thought about it the more she realised that it was totally in keeping with his caring nature.

Calmer now, she sat up and straightened her shoulders, feeling as if she'd just shed a great weight.

'Do you think your solicitor would have time to see me at short notice?' she enquired with new resolution in her voice. 'I'm free all day tomorrow, and I wouldn't mind waiting if it's difficult to fit me in.'

'A case of—if it's got to be done, let's get it over with?' Noah smiled. 'Give me a minute and I'll find out. . .' He consulted his diary, then reached for the phone and tapped out the series of numbers for a connection.

A few minutes' conversation with someone who was obviously a personal friend brought the news that his friend would be free to see her at nine o'clock the following morning.

When Noah relayed the time and the address of the

office a squadron of butterflies took off inside Helen's stomach, and she felt the colour leave her face. The first step had been taken, and by the time the whole strategy was over who knew what her world would look like?

'Don't worry,' Noah soothed. 'The whole process is quite painless, and Gerry is utterly trustworthy. Even if anyone from Q'ran traces anything back this far, they won't get any further.'

'Will you tell your friend everything?'

'I think that would be a good idea, don't you? Then at least there'll be one person in England who'll know the whole story while we're out of the country.'

Helen glanced down at her watch and stood up, conscious that her knees were somewhat shaky.

'It's time I went back to the ward,' she announced and, hearing the matching tremor in her voice, drew in a calming breath and straightened her shoulders before she continued. 'Thank you for spending so much time sorting out my problems, but I've got a poor staff nurse starving to death while she waits for me to return so I must get going.'

'Shall I pick you up tomorrow morning or have you got your own car?' Noah had stood up too and seemed to be closer than ever, apparently taking up what little space there was in the room.

'I'll make my own way there,' Helen confirmed in a voice which still wasn't as steady as she would have liked, then almost stumbled in her haste to leave the suddenly claustrophobic confines of Noah's office.

'That wasn't so bad, now, was it?' Noah pronounced heartily as they stepped out onto the pavement in front of Gerry's office.

'I suppose not,' Helen agreed faintly, trying to be polite

when, in actual fact, she felt as if she'd narrowly survived being flattened by a steamroller. Just lately it seemed as if every time she came anywhere near Noah Kincaid the same thing happened.

A brief flare of anger at the unwelcome sensation of helplessness had her whirling to face him, her heart thumping with agitation.

'Why didn't you warn me that you'd organised for all these other arrangements to be made?' she demanded hoarsely. 'Don't I have *any* say in what's going on?'

Noah captured her elbow in one hand and urged her towards the small adjoining car park, while Helen fought to control the fresh surge of emotions caused by the unexpected physical contact.

She'd hardly begun to deal with the shock of finding out that Noah's good friend Gerry was the stunningly beautiful Geraldine, with a river of dark auburn hair and legs up to her armpits.

When she looked back on the moment of discovery Helen was horribly afraid that if either of them had cared to look, she would have been caught standing in the doorway to the elegant office with her mouth open in shock as the model-perfect woman had twined herself around Noah and begun to practise mouth-to-mouth resuscitation on him.

She was still stunned by the sharp twist of jealousy which had tied her stomach in knots, even though she had no reason to feel it.

Helen remembered that when Noah had made his offer of help he had asked her if she had an alternative male waiting in the wings, but she hadn't even thought about asking if he had some female friend who would object to the arrangement. Now she had found out.

Geraldine's efficient completion of the task Noah had set her had been coloured by the barely veiled disdain which the elegant solicitor had shown towards his companion.

Now Helen found herself horribly aware of the warmth of his hand as he led her towards his car, in spite of the fact that she was trying to nurture a shield of anger to deflect the growing attraction which had begun to plague her.

'Just a minute. . .' Helen tried to jerk her elbow out of his grasp, but his long surgeon's fingers were too strong to let her slip away that easily. She tried again when he aimed the electronic gadget on his key-ring at the door and opened it for her. 'I don't *want* to get in your car,' she objected—with all the sophistication of a sulky child—and wasn't really surprised when he ignored her.

'We need to talk,' he muttered through gritted teeth, and for the first time Helen noticed that the muscles at the corners of his jaw were knotted tightly. 'You have a choice,' he continued as he deliberately took his hand away from her elbow. 'We can talk out here—where the whole world is welcome to eavesdrop—or you can get inside and we'll conduct the conversation with a degree of privacy and decorum.'

Silently Helen turned and slid into the leather-clad luxury of the deeply upholstered seat, stonily staring straight ahead as he clicked the door shut beside her.

She didn't need to watch him circle the back of the car to know that his long legs were covering the ground towards his own door with the leashed power of an angry predator.

'Right, now,' he began tautly as he twisted to face her across the shrinking space between them. 'Suppose you tell me what all this nonsense is about. I thought we'd already decided what we were going to do about your paperwork.'

'In principle,' Helen agreed sharply, refusing to do more than turn her head towards him. 'What I didn't expect was to come here and find that you'd already got the whole thing set up, including a meeting with the registrar, and that you'd got your girlfriend to make all the arrangements.'

'My...what?' Noah's voice and expression showed his shock.

'Oh, come on!' Helen scoffed. 'Did you think I was too dumb to realise why she was treating me like that? Did you forget to explain to her that it's just a brief marriage of convenience?'

'I think *I* must be the dumb one here,' Noah murmured, sounding almost stunned. 'What on earth makes you think Gerry's my girlfriend? I certainly didn't say it. . .'

Helen watched as a layer of colour heightened the crest of his cheek-bones, and suddenly wondered if she'd made a mistake.

'Well, *I've* certainly never greeted a stranger that fervently,' she said stiffly, once again remembering the way the tall redhead had plastered herself all over Noah. 'And if she wasn't your girlfriend, why was she trying so hard to make you change your mind?'

'I can think of several reasons,' Noah said, his calm voice evidence that he'd already regained his composure. 'Including the fact that she knows I've recently inherited a large chunk of family assets in the Channel Islands and she might have been trying to protect my interests.'

'Or her own,' Helen added snidely, knowing intuitively that Gerry was far more interested in Noah the man than in any amount of property or money he might possess.

'She was an old friend of my wife's,' he said quietly, and, out of the corner of her eye, Helen saw his hands clench tightly on the steering-wheel. 'I've known her for years,' he continued, his voice strangely empty. 'And in all that time there's never been anything. . .' He shrugged dismissively.

Not by *her* choice, Helen thought as the situation suddenly became clear. Gerry-the-good-friend would far rather be Gerry-the-wife or even Gerry-the-lover, but Noah hadn't shown any interest. Not only that, but he had just asked Gerry-the-solicitor to arrange the paperwork to enable him to marry someone else.

A strange warmth spread through her, and Helen was conscious that the steel band which had tightened itself around her chest had suddenly disappeared.

'So, do you want to keep the appointment with the registrar?' Noah demanded quietly. 'It's up to you.'

Helen breathed deeply as her shoulders straightened and her head came up proudly.

'Yes, please,' she said calmly, grateful for his display of patience. 'I'm sorry about the last-minute histrionics.'

'It was quite revealing,' he said with a badly concealed smile. 'The unflappable Sister Morrisey in a complete tizzy!'

'Not any more.' Her voice was firm with resolve. 'I'm going to be everlastingly grateful to you for finding the way to give me the chance to see Nash. I promise I won't let you down.'

There was a pause before Noah leant forward to start the engine and Helen thought she heard him sigh, but by the time she looked across at him his expression was as calm as ever.

# CHAPTER FIVE

'You sly thing!' Anne Denton whispered as she leant towards Helen and handed her the small posy of flowers. 'Oh, I think it's *so* romantic!'

Helen smiled wanly as she accepted the spray of deep red rosebuds surrounded by a froth of baby's-breath, half-convinced that she was going to be sick she was so full of nerves. Her head thumped with the start of a monumental headache.

'I'm so glad you asked me to be your witness,' Annie's excited murmur continued. 'I couldn't believe it when Mr. . .when Noah asked me. . .' A pretty pink washed over her cheeks as she glanced across at the tall man, sitting on Helen's other side.

Helen hadn't been able to believe it either.

Without a single word of warning, he'd walked calmly into her office while her staff nurse was sneaking an extra biscuit out of the recently replenished tin and, with one arm wrapped possessively around his bogus fiancée's shoulders, had announced that they'd like Annie to be part of the wedding party.

Helen hadn't been able to control her gasp of shock, but at least the sound had been covered by Annie's squeal of surprise. It had only been the swift squeeze he'd given her which had stopped her jaw from hitting her knees.

Now, three short days later, they were waiting their turn in the little ante-room, and the silent sweep-hand on the bold-faced clock was measuring the few remaining minutes.

'Last chance to make a run for it!' Peter Keenan murmured cheekily, leaning forward to look at her around Noah's broad shoulder.

Helen's smile was a little more natural in response to his freckle-faced good humour, but she wondered how long Peter would have been smiling if he'd realised that he'd just voiced her own thoughts.

'Go and find your own girl,' Noah growled as he glanced down at Helen's pale face and shaky hands. 'This one's mine.'

To her surprise, he wrapped his arm around her in the same way he had in her office but this time it just felt comforting and secure, and she was filled with the urge to rest her aching head on the width of his broad shoulder.

'He's right, you know,' Noah breathed carefully so that neither of their companions could overhear his words. 'All you have to do is say you've changed your mind. . .'

Helen gazed up into deep blue eyes and wondered anew at the man's generosity. If she were to do as he suggested, the story would be all around the hospital faster than a virus and would lose nothing in the telling.

She would be giving in to her deep-rooted fears, but she would be leaving him with the devastating embarrassment of being jilted at the very last minute—and it wasn't as if he even *wanted* to be married to her in the first place.

Suddenly she realised just how much trust he was placing in her sense of fair play. He had offered his name as a solution to her dilemma, without expecting anything in return other than that she should play her part in convincing their colleagues that this was a genuine marriage.

He met her eyes without flinching, silently letting her know that he was leaving the final decision in her hands, and suddenly she knew deep inside that—as much as he was trusting her—he was equally worthy of her trust.

'No, thank you,' she breathed softly in return, the lightening in her heart tempting her to tease a little. 'You're not getting out of it that easily. . .'

Before Noah could do more than smile in response the door at the other end of the room opened, and a sober-suited gentleman beckoned them through.

Helen stood up on shaky knees, grateful for Noah's support as they walked forward together.

'You may now kiss your bride. . .' the registrar prompted, the words emerging through the haze which seemed to have surrounded Helen throughout the brief ceremony.

Suddenly her heart began to pound and she felt as though she couldn't breathe as his hands cupped her shoulders and turned her towards him.

Helen found her eyes riveted on the single deep red rosebud in the buttonhole of his suit, a perfect match for the elegant arrangement she clutched tightly in her suddenly clammy hands.

Time seemed to disappear as she felt the touch of his fingers against her cheek, coaxing her chin up until her blue-grey eyes met his quizzical gaze.

'Just a kiss,' he whispered softly, the gentle smile on his face easing her tension slightly even as she watched his lips moving inexorably towards her.

Just a kiss. . .

How could she have known that there would be no such thing as 'just a kiss' from Noah Kincaid?

At the first touch of his lips she was aware of a strange

sensation—almost like electricity—which flowed between the two of them, her eyelids closing as if she needed to concentrate totally on the surprisingly soft warmth of his mouth.

Almost before she had time to chart the glow which began to spread outwards from the contact it was broken.

Unaccountably bereft, she opened heavy eyes just in time to watch him raise her hands from their position trapped between them, her forgotten posy still tightly gripped in white-knuckled hands.

Bemused, she watched as he separated the left hand from its death grip and bent his head over it to kiss the ring he'd so recently placed on her fourth finger.

'Ah!' She heard Annie sigh somewhere behind her. 'It's just so romantic. . .' Out of the corner of her eye Helen saw Peter offering her a large white handkerchief.

The final formalities were completed in just a few minutes and, almost before Helen had gathered her wits about her, they were being ushered out of another door to make way for the next couple, already waiting in the ante-room.

'I hope the two of you will have time to join us for a celebratory drink,' Noah began as the four of them walked towards the small car park.

Helen's heart sank. For all her nervousness about being alone with Noah, she wasn't certain how long she would be able to keep up her end of the deception—especially in the company of observant people like Peter and Annie.

Just as Peter glanced at his watch and frowned there was the familiar sound of a pager.

'Mine,' Noah said with a grimace, and switched it off with one hand while he activated the gadget to allow him access to his car phone.

Leaving Noah to conduct what was obviously a work-related conversation, Helen turned towards their companions to thank them for their company. She was just in time to witness a strangely conspiratorial glance between the two of them.

Stifling the speculation that she might be witnessing the start of a new relationship, she smiled and offered her hand to Peter.

'Thanks for standing up with Noah today,' she started politely, then gasped when she found herself wrapped in an exuberant bear-hug.

'Congratulations, Mrs Kincaid,' he said enthusiastically, and swung her off her feet and into a high-spirited circle. 'I couldn't be more delighted—even though I think you chose the wrong man!' He kissed her noisily on the cheek before he put her feet back on the ground.

'Unhand my woman!' Noah ordered as he switched off the phone. 'I only turn my back for a moment and look what he's up to. . .!'

'Oh, Noah!' Annie said through happy tears as she threw her arms around his shoulders. 'You couldn't have chosen anyone better. I'm sure you and Helen are going to be very happy!'

'I think you're right,' he agreed, wrapping a friendly arm around her shoulders as she used Peter's handkerchief again—his eyes an even darker blue as they met Helen's across the intervening space. 'Unfortunately that call means that I've got to go back to the hospital straight away, so we'll have to go out for that celebration another day.'

'No problem.' Peter dismissed the postponement surprisingly airily. 'If you could give Annie and I a lift to the hospital at the same time, it would save us the price of a taxi. . .'

Now that there was a good chance that she was going to be facing some of her colleagues on the hospital staff, Helen found she was wishing that she could have spent longer in the more restricted company of their two friends.

Pete and Annie had opted to sit in the back of the car and had apparently found instant common ground, as they murmured throughout the journey back to St Augustine's.

Helen found herself turning her little posy round and round in her hands, as though somewhere between the dark smooth elegance of the deep red rosebuds and the dainty frothy white of the baby's-breath she could find the answers to all the problems in the universe.

'Chin up,' Noah murmured gently as he covered her chilly, fidgeting hands with one of his far larger and much warmer ones. 'Stage two completed,' he said cryptically, and she realised suddenly that she'd almost forgotten the reason behind the afternoon's events.

Unfortunately she wasn't certain whether the emotions that flooded her were relief that she was another step closer to seeing her son, or disappointment that it had obviously been at the forefront of Noah's mind.

As she sat, silently watching as he expertly manoeuvred the car into his allotted space, she was startled to realise how much she had wanted him to say something... anything...to let her know that he had been as moved by the ceremony as she had been and that, in spite of the circumstances, he was glad that the two of them had decided to...

Stupid! she castigated herself sternly as she opened the car door without waiting for Noah to walk around. She knew that they had both gone into the arrangement for one reason—to make it safe for her to find out if Nash was well cared for and happy.

What on earth did she think she was doing? Was she hoping that Noah would tell her she looked beautiful? Tell her how happy he was to be married to her? Was she really stupid enough to expect a marriage of convenience to have changed into the love-match of the century?

'Would you rather wait in the car while I find out what the problem is?' Noah suggested, and Helen was half-afraid that she must have given her thoughts away somehow.

'You're not condemning her to hours of waiting in a car park, are you?' Peter teased. 'You know very well that there's no telling how long you'll be. At least she can have a cup of coffee if she comes up with you.'

Noah shrugged, and Helen found his apparent indifference almost a relief. At least he hadn't picked up on her strange ambivalence towards him.

The four of them were just passing the doors to the ground floor day-room when they were swung open. Before Helen realised what was happening she and Noah had been shepherded into the room by Peter and Annie.

'Surprise. . .!'

'Congratulations. . .!'

There was a sudden burst of noise and the two of them were surrounded by well-wishers.

'Thought you could keep it secret, did you?' Noah's opposite number taunted as he approached with two brimming glasses in his hands. 'You ought to know what the grapevine's like in this place!'

'The worst part has been trying to keep everything a secret,' Annie admitted, almost bubbling over with the excitement of having been in on the surprise from the start. 'Everyone's been fighting to get some time off to be here.'

'It certainly seems as if they've succeeded,' Noah said drily as he gazed around at a room full of colleagues. 'It looks as if the entire staff of the whole hospital is here!'

When she had realised what was going on Helen had shrunk back into the shelter of Noah's much larger body, uncomfortably wishing that there was some way she could disappear completely.

'Did you know about this?' she muttered, feeling as if her cheeks would never cool down again. 'Did you know what they were planning?'

'If I had I'd have avoided it like the plague,' he replied under cover of the happy chatter. 'I hate surprises—that's probably why they resorted to telling me I had a new patient to look at!'

'That's what the phone call was about when we came out of the register office?'

He nodded briefly. 'It was the only thing guaranteed not to make me suspicious of something like this. Just wait till I get my hands on Peter and Annie!'

'Come on, you two.' As if he knew they were talking about him, Peter's warm Irish accent hailed them from the other side of a white-frosted cake—both hands beckoning them to come closer. 'You've got the rest of your lives to murmur sweet nothings to each other. It's time to cut the cake!'

There was a surge of bodies which carried them forward, and Helen nearly had her feet swept out from under her until Noah wrapped a protective arm around her shoulders and held her tightly against himself.

'Are you all right?' he was quick to enquire, his expression quite concerned. 'Let's get this bedlam over with quickly and make our escape. . .'

Surrounded by laughter and jokes, the two of them were

proudly positioned in front of the beautiful cake, and cameras flashed as they were presented with an enormous knife.

'The best the kitchens could supply,' Peter quipped. 'I didn't think your usual little blades would be quite up to the job, sharp though they are!'

As Noah's hand wrapped warmly over hers around the handle of the knife Helen found herself mentally replaying the little tradition she'd been taught by one of her foster-mothers. As the knife sank out of sight she closed her eyes briefly as she tried to think of the three wishes she would like fulfilled by the luck of the cake.

Her first wish was easy—to find Nash in good health. The second was something she'd been dreaming about ever since Mahmoud had engineered the kidnapping—to have her son with her again. The third wish arrived from nowhere and snapped her eyes wide open with shock. What on earth had made her put Noah Kincaid and love into the same thought and turn them into a wish?

'Speech! Speech!' came the chorus as soon as the first slice was cut and the knife had been handed over for willing hands to complete the task.

A circle opened up around the two of them and the noise died away to a gentle murmur as every eye turned towards them.

Noah reached for Helen's hand, and she wasn't certain whether the trembling she felt was just her own, or whether he was afflicted too, and she tightened her fingers around his much longer ones.

As if surprised by the gesture, Noah glanced down at her—his eyes deeply blue as he captured her gaze for several long seconds before clearing his throat.

'Unaccustomed as I am. . .' he began and was greeted

with jeers so that he had to begin again. 'I won't ask what's happened to all the duty rosters but, on behalf of Helen and myself, I want to thank every one of you for being here today. We couldn't have had a better send-off—or a warmer one—for the start of our marriage.'

'How about a kiss?' Peter called.

'I'm sorry, Pete, but you're not my type,' Noah dead-panned to raucous laughter. 'And, anyway, I don't think my wife would like it—she might get jealous!'

In spite of the round of laughter which the repartee provoked, several others took up the chorus, demanding that he kiss his new bride. He turned towards her.

'It looks as if we're not going to get away until we've complied, so how about it?' he murmured in a husky voice.

Helen was entranced by the strangely shy expression on his face, and found it easy to smile her agreement.

'I suppose we could always look on it as a practice session,' she suggested lightly, to cover up the fact that her pulse was already beating frantically in anticipation. 'Before we go to Q'ran. . .'

The hands which had gently cupped her shoulders froze in position and the tender warmth which had filled his eyes changed until he looked almost angry, but before Helen could analyse what had brought about the startling change his lips were meeting hers and her brain ceased to function.

This was no tentative exploration.

This kiss allowed no leeway for the fact that they had only kissed once before, and that time had been a restrained meeting of lips in front of the registrar and three witnesses.

This time his lips and tongue demanded and, after her initial surprise, she was powerless to resist.

This time it was only the chorus of whistles and appreciative cat-calls which brought the two of them sharply back to the realisation of where they were, and Helen hid her face against Noah's shoulder to conceal the fiery evidence of her embarrassment.

'If. . .' Noah paused to clear his throat and began again in a husky voice. 'If you'll all forgive us, I think it's time we were going. . .'

His words were drowned by another chorus of laughter and well-meaning comments from his male colleagues but he didn't speak again, restricting himself to smiling and waving his farewells as he guided Helen out of the door and into the relative silence of the corridor.

'Helen. . .' he began hesitantly, but she couldn't bear the thought that someone might follow them out into the corridor and perhaps overhear Noah apologise for the unfortunate display they had just provided.

'Let's get out of here,' she interrupted swiftly as she slid her hand out from his delaying hold and set off along the corridor. 'Quick. Before anyone thinks of following us out to the car. . .'

'Hang on a minute. . .' His much longer legs meant that he had no difficulty catching up with her. 'Actually, I was going to suggest that we went across to my room.'

'Your room. . .?' Helen swallowed to try to ease the sudden tightness in her throat. 'What. . .? Why?'

'I thought it would be more convenient if we weren't too far away from work in case they have to call me to a genuine case.' His lips curved into a wry smile. 'I couldn't manage to get an appointment for the ceremony, except when I was on call. We need to sort out some of the basic logistics and we just haven't had time to talk.'

Helen had to admit that he was right. Ever since she'd accepted his offer of marriage the day seemed to have

shrunk to half the number of hours, and the amount of
work to fit into the time seemed to have doubled.

She sighed and bit her lip. One thing that hadn't had
time to do more than flit through her mind was the possibility that he was trying to lure her up to his room for romantic
purposes. They just didn't have that sort of relationship. . .

'I hope you're going to offer me something to drink
when we get there,' she commented with an attempt at
nonchalance as she began to walk beside him in the direction of the accommodation block.

'What did you have in mind? I'm afraid I didn't think
of getting any champagne. . .'

'I'd prefer tea or coffee,' she admitted honestly. 'I've
never drunk a lot and champagne gives me a terrible
headache.'

'I wondered why you didn't drink any when they proposed the toast,' he commented. 'I wondered if you felt
it was a bit hypocritical, in view of the reason you
married me.'

'I wondered the same thing,' she said with a surreptitious glance up at him. 'Then I realised that you didn't
drink yours because you're still on call.'

'Not only beautiful but bright, too,' he complimented
as he drew her to a halt outside the last door in a row
of identical dark wood panels in the purpose-built
accommodation block.

Helen knew that his words were just a throwaway line,
but that didn't stop her heart giving an extra beat at the
pleasure she felt that he thought she was beautiful.

In spite of the strange circumstances, she'd felt that
she owed it to both of them to look her best, and as she
entered his room and turned to face him she caught sight
of their images in the mirror over the corner basin and

could see the two of them together for the first time.

His dark suit was quietly elegant and fitted him so well that it must have been individually tailored to the breadth of his shoulders and the length of his back.

He closed the door and walked towards her. The expression in his eyes as they skimmed over her told her that the time and money spent on the fluid lines of the ivory silk dress she wore had been well worth it, as had the appointment with the hairdresser to coil her hair into such a becoming style.

'I mean it,' he said quietly, almost as though he had read her doubting thoughts. 'You looked beautiful today. I was proud to have you standing at my side.'

Helen felt the warmth creep up her cheeks when she realised how sincere he was.

'No one's ever said that before,' she whispered as she felt the hot prickle of tears behind her eyes. She turned towards the window while she fought for control.

No one had ever been so complimentary before—not even her husband. Oh, he'd admired her hair. In fact, he'd been fascinated by the golden shimmer of it as it hung nearly to her waist. But she'd learned within the first twenty-four hours of her marriage that he'd only been attracted to certain aspects of her outer appearance.

'Hey! I'm sorry. . .' Noah murmured as he joined her in her contemplation of the straggly shrubbery bordering the car park. 'If this is the reaction caused by a compliment, I promise not to do it again!'

Helen gave a watery chuckle, brought back from the brink of tears by his nonsense.

'I'm glad you approved,' she said with a steadier voice. 'I wanted to look good because I had an idea that Peter and Annie would be reporting back, but I had no idea that everyone would be getting in on the act!'

'I suppose it was all to the good,' Noah agreed. 'It won't matter if anyone *does* make enquiries now. The whole hospital will be able to give them chapter and verse about our wedding day.'

'Do you think the authorities in Q'ran will ask questions?' The idea could still chill her blood.

'Not unless we do something silly which makes them question our story,' he said firmly. 'All we have to do is behave like any normal married couple, and there'll be no problem. Don't borrow trouble,' he added persuasively as he went across to the tiny kitchenette in one corner.

Helen drew in a deep breath and let it out slowly, calmed by his air of certainty and the very normality of watching him fill the kettle and switch it on.

'Well, I don't know what you've got planned for the rest of the day but, after nearly a week of sleepless nights, I finally feel as if I'll sleep well tonight.' She lifted a small stack of professional journals off the only comfortable-looking chair and deposited them on the tidy surface of the small desk before she collapsed gratefully into its support.

'That's something we have to talk about,' Noah said, still occupied with his task in the corner. When Helen looked towards him all she could see was the hint of darker colour around the back of his neck.

'Oh?'

'The matter of where you're going to sleep. . .' he prompted in a slightly husky voice as he turned to face her across the room.

'Oh, that's no problem. As you're on call I can easily get a taxi back to my flat.'

It wasn't until the ensuing silence seemed to stretch

into infinity that Helen thought about the significance of what she'd said, and her pulse rate doubled.

'Oh,' she said again, but this time it wasn't a question.

'You've realised the problem,' Noah said quietly as he walked forward with the two steaming mugs in his hands. 'There are still three weeks left until we're due to leave for Q'ran and we daren't do anything to cast doubt on our story.'

'But. . .' Helen stopped, unable to find any words; unable even to find the strength to lift her hand to take the mug he was offering.

'Knowing what nursing salaries are like, I don't suppose your flat is anything much bigger than a rabbit hutch?' he queried.

'Not much bigger than this,' Helen confirmed with a quick glance around the spartan room. 'Except I've got my own shower and the kitchenette is a bit more comprehensive.'

'What about the bed?' Noah asked bluntly.

'S-single,' she stammered as she realised the way his questions were going. 'And the settee is just a two-seater, so neither of us could sleep on it.'

Finally she managed to take the proffered mug, needing to wrap both hands around it in spite of the fact that the room was perfectly warm—totally conscious of the fact that he was standing so close to her while they were discussing their sleeping arrangements.

Her tension eased slightly when he moved away from her, taking his own mug and sitting down on the edge of the bed.

'So that leaves us with the choice of staying here or moving into a hotel for the next three weeks.'

'And apart from the fact that would be unnecessarily

'expensive. . .' Helen began in a worried tone.

'It could also raise questions,' Noah continued calmly. 'And that would be a shame after the good impression we made today.'

'What about your house?' she suggested tentatively. 'There's plenty of room. . .'

'No,' he broke in sharply and then, as she watched warily, he drew in a steadying breath. 'I'm sorry,' he murmured.

'I'm sorry. . .' Helen began, her words running over his apology. 'I didn't mean to presume. . .'

His expression silenced her, a strange mixture of anger and sadness before he retreated behind his usual inscrutability.

'Apart from the fact that I don't want to take you to the house where. . .where I was less than happy,' he began hesitantly, 'we couldn't stay there because there isn't any furniture left upstairs.'

'What? But why?'

She caught a glimpse of uncertainty in his expression before he straightened his shoulders and replied honestly, 'Because I gave it all away to charity. I knew I wouldn't ever use it again.'

Helen heard the echo of sorrow in the words, and had to drag her thoughts away from his unhappy memories and back to their own problem.

'But. . . Here. . .?' Helen bit her lip, forcing herself to gaze down into her mug when her eyes were drawn with some fatal fascination towards the bed on which Noah was sitting.

'It's my own bed,' Noah offered, almost as if he'd been reading her mind. 'I'm too big to cope with the single one they provided.'

The hint of laughter in his voice drew her eyes towards him, and she couldn't help the way she measured his height and breadth nor the answering chuckle caused by the mental image of Noah cramped into her own single bed—let alone sharing it with her.

'So, have we made a decision?' he enquired, his voice as calm and even as if he was asking whether she wanted another drink.

'I. . .I suppose so,' Helen agreed, pressing her lips tightly together when she heard how hesitant she sounded.

'Helen. . .?' He paused, waiting until she looked at him before he continued. 'You do know that you haven't got anything to worry about, don't you?'

'W-worry?' she repeated breathlessly.

'You can trust me,' he stated firmly. 'I know you've only married me because you're afraid of what your ex-husband might do to you if he recognised your name, but you won't have to worry that I'll be taking advantage of the situation. We might be forced to share a bed, but you won't be forced into anything else.'

His direct gaze left her in no doubt as to what he was talking about and she blushed furiously, cursing her adolescent reaction to even an oblique reference to sex.

She straightened her shoulders, determined that he wasn't going to take her for a simpering ninny. She'd managed to survive an attempt on her life, and she'd been working and planning ever since to rescue her son. No prudish sensibilities were going to stop her now.

'I know that, Noah,' she said, pleased by the new calm strength in her voice. 'I know I can trust you.'

'Helen. . .'

'You've been wonderful—so helpful in working out a way for me to go to Q'ran to see Nash—even though there's nothing in it for you. I'll never be able to thank you enough for what you're doing.'

Now it was Noah's turn to look abashed, and just when Helen would have liked to meet his eyes to convince him of her sincerity he seemed inordinately interested in the nubbly design of the bedspread and refused to look at her.

It was almost a relief when the uncomfortable silence between them was broken by the sound of his pager. As she watched him reach across for the mobile phone he'd brought in from the car she felt as if she were drawing in her first deep breath for hours.

'Right.' His deep voice broke into her musings as he brought the call to an end. 'I should be with you in about five minutes.'

She watched him telescope the antenna away as he turned towards her, and her eyes were drawn to the elegance of his long-fingered hands.

'Helen. . .?' His tone let her know that he was repeating himself. 'You'll need to collect a few things from your flat to tide you over until we can make more permanent plans. Here.' He held out a small bunch of keys. 'You might as well take my car so you'll have plenty of space.'

'Oh, but. . .' Helen was horrified at the thought of driving his expensive car. 'What if I have an accident?'

'Just take it steady and you'll be all right—I trust you,' he said with a broad grin and a surprisingly boyish wink. 'Sorry to have to leave you like this, but I'll see you later.'

He paused in the middle of the room for a second, almost as if he was undecided about something, then shook his head, sketched a brief wave and left.

'Well,' Helen breathed as her pulse rate slowly returned to normal. For just one minute she'd thought he was going to come over and kiss her goodbye, but the worst part of the fact that he hadn't was that she wasn't sure whether she was relieved or disappointed at his decision.

'You've got three weeks to get your brain sorted out, my girl,' she muttered aloud into the empty room. 'Three weeks before you're going to be in Q'ran, and any slip-ups there could mean danger for the whole team—not just you.'

With the echo of her own admonition ringing in her ears, she grabbed her bag and made for the door. She'd learnt the hard way that one sure-fire method for stopping her brain from wandering off into the realms of speculation was to keep herself busy, and the sooner she did it the better.

# CHAPTER SIX

'WE'LL be landing in about ten minutes,' Noah's deep voice said in Helen's ear as she gazed out of the window, and she was dragged sharply back to her surroundings.

She'd been daydreaming about their trip to Q'ran and now, while she gathered up her few items of hand-luggage, she had to adjust to the fact that they were just completing a short-haul flight between London and Cornwall on what was to be her first 'away' case with the team.

A week and a half had passed since she had moved into Noah's cramped accommodation, and it hadn't taken long before they'd both realised that the situation was fraught with difficulties.

Working together wasn't a problem. Helen had insisted that they should continue exactly as they had before their marriage, with only her change of name to show that anything was different.

They'd had to put up with some teasing from the other staff for the first few days, but that had long since died away in the face of their calm attitude.

It was the tension which began mounting once they both arrived back at his room that was wearing on their nerves, and a quick glance at Noah while he perused a sheaf of papers confirmed the same story of strain and shadows that she had seen on her own face this morning.

They had both tried hard—perhaps too hard—to give each other space, but when it reached the level that the two of them were finding all sorts of excuses to spend as little time together as possible it had reached the limit.

That telling view in the mirror this morning had given Helen the impetus she needed. It was difficult for the two of them to talk seriously at St Augustine's without the possibility that some other member of staff might overhear, even in the apparent privacy of the staff accommodation, but this trip could be the ideal solution.

They were booked into a hotel near the hospital, and she was determined that at some stage over the next few days the two of them were going to find the time to thrash out their problems.

If nothing else, she knew that the accommodation at the hotel would allow the two of them a bit of breathing space as their rooms had been booked before their marriage.

They would have to do something, she thought anxiously, flicking another glance up at Noah's preoccupied expression. If they couldn't find some way to present themselves as a united couple the whole scheme, which revolved round their visit to Q'ran, would fall apart about their ears.

She would do anything to avoid that. *Nothing* must be allowed to interfere with her chance of seeing Nash.

'Are we due to go straight to the hospital?' she enquired as Noah finally tucked the papers away in his briefcase and stowed it safely under his seat preparatory to landing.

'It will depend on the transport from the airport, but I believe the flight was chosen to get us in with enough time to drop our belongings off first. We might even have a few minutes to freshen up a bit after the journey.'

He smiled, but Helen's heart tightened when she saw how tired he was looking.

She knew that she hadn't slept well in the last couple of weeks, but Noah had been so considerate of her feelings that he'd engineered his hours so that they were rarely off duty together. When she'd added it up she'd realised that since their marriage they'd actually spent less than a dozen chaste hours together in the confines of his oversized bed, most of them while she was soundly asleep.

The transfer from plane to taxi was easy when undertaken by a seasoned traveller like Noah and, after a pleasantly swift journey through lush countryside, they soon reached the surprisingly compact west country city and were deposited at the entrance of one of the better hotels.

'You have reservations for us in the name of Kincaid,' Noah said confidently as they reached the desk.

'Ah, yes,' the smartly dressed gentleman agreed with a broad smile as he tapped keys to access the relevant information on the computer. 'Mr and Mrs Kincaid in the honeymoon suite.'

'What. . .?' Helen gasped, then blushed furiously when every eye seemed to focus on her with indulgent smiles.

'When was the booking changed?' Noah asked, his deep voice sounding strangely cold and tight.

'Just a couple of hours ago, sir. A gentleman rang the alteration through from London.' The receptionist was beginning to look worried. 'I'm sorry, sir. Has it caused a problem?'

Noah turned halfway towards Helen and raised a surreptitious eyebrow.

In a flash she knew what he was asking—and the reasons. If Peter had taken the trouble to change their reservations from single rooms to the honeymoon suite they could be certain that he would want a full account of their luxurious stay in Cornwall, and they could hardly do that if they changed the reservations back again.

With an almost imperceptible nod of her head she acquiesced, and watched silently while Noah signed the register and accepted the key to their room.

'So much for our breathing space,' he murmured cryptically before the lift door enclosed them in the confined space with other passengers. Helen's eyes flew up to meet the wry expression in his.

'Are you a mind-reader? That's exactly what I was thinking,' she replied under her breath, and suddenly the heavy load on her shoulders seemed to lighten. She hadn't realised that he felt the same way, but now she did it would make it easier for her to bring up her concerns for their trip to Q'ran.

'What a gorgeous room!' she exclaimed spontaneously as they entered the spacious reception area. 'I was terrified when I heard it was the honeymoon suite that it would be one of those aggressively *pink* rooms, but this is lovely.'

She stood in the middle and and turned in a circle as she surveyed the restful mixture of ivory, deep peach and soft green, with large comfortable-looking upholstered chairs in front of a television set and, in front of the windows, a dining-table for two framed by sumptuously draped curtains.

'At least the decorator made some concessions for the fact that one half of a honeymoon couple is male,' Noah commented as he went exploring.

'Lovely big bathroom.' His voice emerged from behind one of the doors leading off the reception room. 'And it's got the first hotel bath I've ever seen that looks long enough for me to lie down in.'

Helen chuckled silently at the memory of the standard-sized bath back at the hospital. It had never occurred to her that Noah must have his knees bent almost under his nose when he sat in it!

The thought of Noah's naked body in any bath at all was enough to have her pulse skipping, so she hurriedly made her way towards the other door to explore the sleeping arrangements.

'Oh, my. . .!' Speechless, she stood in the doorway and stared.

'Obviously they let another designer loose in this room,' Noah murmured, his deep voice just by her ear.

'Obviously.' Helen forced the word out through her clenched teeth, trying desperately to sound normal but— from the clammy feeling of her skin—she knew that she must have gone deathly white.

She'd never expected that the room would look like *this*—a scene out of her worst nightmares.

'Do you think Rudolph Valentino's hiding in there?' Noah whispered conspiratorially. 'It's a setting straight out of Arabian Nights. . .'

As Helen looked at the circular bed draped and swagged with enough muslin to furnish a marquee she felt like gagging, and her knees trembled so badly that she had to lean against the doorframe for support.

'Helen. . .? Helen!' There was sharp concern in his voice but she barely heard it through the roaring sound in her ears. She was almost mesmerised by the awful sight in front of her, but out of the corner of her eye she saw Noah's hand move as he reached out towards her.

Helen flinched away from him abruptly, unable to bear the thought of him touching her, and she was conscious that his hand froze in mid-air.

'Helen?' he repeated softly, and she could feel his eyes

watching her intently. 'Are you all right? Is there anything I can do?'

She dragged her horrified gaze away from the bed and saw the dark disquiet in his eyes as she cowered away from him against the wall.

'I'm s-sorry,' she whispered brokenly as she covered her face with both her shaking hands. 'Oh, God, I'm sorry, Noah. I didn't mean to... It wasn't you...' She began to sob.

'Oh, Helen. Don't...' he murmured. 'Tell me what I can do to help...'

'Oh, N-noah,' she hiccuped as she lowered her hands and peered out at him through tear-filled eyes as she wrapped her arms around herself.

He was standing quite still, as if he expected his slightest move to tip her into full-blown panic, and she only had to look at the expression on his face to recognise his genuine concern.

'P-please, Noah, just h-hold me...' she begged raggedly.

His arms encircled her almost tentatively at first, as though he was afraid she would reject the contact, but when she turned towards him and buried her face against his shoulder—her arms wrapped tightly around his waist as she burrowed into his arms like a terrified animal—he tightened his grasp until he was supporting almost all her weight.

It was several minutes before the sobbing died away and she regained enough control of herself to lift her head, but when she tried to straighten away from him he tightened his arm persuasively around her shoulders.

'Stay still a minute longer,' he murmured. 'Just catch your breath.'

Gratefully Helen allowed her head to return to its resting place on his shoulder again, and for the first time in her life she felt as if she'd come home. She dragged in a shuddering breath and with it drew in the mixture of scents which signified Noah—the smell of the crisply laundered cotton of his shirt, the fresh smell of soap lingering on his skin, but most of all an indefinable musky warmth which belonged only to him.

'Do you want to sit down?' he suggested when her breathing had slowed and become nearly smooth again, and she nodded reluctantly, realising that it meant she would lose her place in his arms.

Straightening, she turned away from him and made her way over to the pair of deeply upholstered armchairs.

'Wait a minute,' he directed as she went to lower herself into the nearest one, and proceeded to sit down in it himself and tug her onto his lap.

Surprise made her hold herself stiffly for a minute but soon she couldn't resist the temptation to relax into his comforting embrace and they subsided into silence.

'Are you ready to tell me what that was all about?' he prompted softly, his breath puffing gently over her skin and tickling her with tendrils of hair.

She sighed deeply as she thought about the origins of her fear, and then told herself that this wasn't the time to tell him. She needed time to come to terms with what had happened in the last half-hour and there wouldn't be enough of it before the two of them were due to leave for the hospital.

The quiet little voice inside her head was more honest, telling her that lack of time wasn't really the problem but rather the fear that maybe she would never be able to tell him.

She pushed the idea into a dark corner and resolved that, in the meantime, at least she would be able to hide behind temporary distractions.

'When are we due at the hospital?' she asked in a voice made husky by her recent tears and then paused, tension returning as she waited for his reaction.

'We should be leaving in half an hour,' he confirmed after a glance at his watch and then, just when she thought he was going to let the subject drop, he tilted her chin with one finger until she was forced to meet the dark blue of his eyes.

'I'm conceding the fact that we haven't got time to talk about it now,' he said with gentle intensity. 'But tonight there'll be plenty of time and, whatever it is, I think you need to talk about it—I know *I* need you to. . .'

The last words were spoken as she scrambled awkwardly to her feet and were said so quietly that Helen wondered if she'd been mistaken.

She turned back to ask him but he was already on his feet.

'Help yourself to the bathroom,' he directed as briskly as if the last few minutes were a figment of her imagination. 'I'll just phone down to confirm the arrangements for our transport.'

Helen grabbed the smallest of the bags, knowing that she'd taken the precaution of packing it with her wash-kit, make-up and a quick change of clothes, and made for the room Noah had so admired.

As she shut the door she had to admit that it was probably the most sumptuous bathroom she'd ever been in, but she didn't really have time to admire it as Noah was waiting to follow her into it. Tonight, she thought, filling her mind with inconsequential nonsense, she'd get a better look at the room when she had time for a wallow in the enormous bath.


'This is a very new cardiac unit, isn't it?' Helen commented to her opposite number as she and Noah were shown through to their temporary headquarters.

'Yes,' confirmed the striking young dark-haired theatre sister. 'For years, if you had a cardiac problem requiring surgery and lived west of Bristol you were forced to travel all the way across the country to London.'

'To London?' Helen's voice was evidence of her shock. 'But that's hundreds of miles away. There must be closer cardiac units than that!'

'Oh, there are,' Jenna Pengelly confirmed wryly in her soft Cornish burr. 'But they were fully occupied with their own patients and didn't have time or space for any coming in from the West Country. The only place with spare beds was London because of the concentration of teaching hospitals there.'

'But what happened to the patients who were too unstable to travel?' Helen's agile mind had immediately hit on the greatest flaw in the old situation. 'And the others—how long did it take for them to recover from the journey once they reached London before they were fit to undergo the operation? And what about their families? How could they visit?'

'If you carry on like that you'll soon come up with all the things we'd been pointing out to the powers-that-be for years,' Jenna said with a humourless laugh. 'You should hear some of the horror stories we've collected.'

'Horror stories?' Helen prompted. In spite of the riveting conversation, her hands were still moving just as swiftly about their task of unpacking and organising Noah's personal equipment and checking off the sterile packs they would need during the first operation.

'Like the lady who was airlifted to London by medical helicopter and died the next day without ever recovering sufficiently from the journey for the surgery to take place. And then there was the doctor who'd had to retire from general practice because of his heart condition, and when the time came for him to go up to London he wasn't fit enough to drive so he set off in a taxi. . .'

'A taxi?' Helen questioned, aghast. 'He went nearly four hundred miles in a taxi?'

'No,' Jenna replied, tight-lipped. 'He was just going past Stonehenge when he had another heart attack.'

'Oh, my God,' Helen breathed. 'Did he die?'

'No. By sheer good luck there was a police car going past, and the terrified taxi-driver managed to flag him down for help.'

'So, now that you've got your own unit, that's all in the past?'

'We're not out of the woods yet because top-flight cardiac surgeons seem to be drawn to London like moths to a flame. They seem to prefer the kudos of saying they work in one of the big London hospitals, rather than in one of the regional centres.'

'But don't they realise that they'll be doing exactly the same operations on the same patients, but without the poor patients being put through a life-threatening obstacle course to get on the table?'

'We're slowly getting the message across but until there's been a lot more decentralisation, with the money and expertise being spread around the country a little more fairly, it looks as if West Country patients are going to continue getting the short end of the stick.'

'Well, you're doing a good job of banging the drum,' Helen confirmed with a smile. 'From now on, when Noah and I are travelling around we can make sure people hear the real story about what's going on in the West Country.'

'It's a shame we can't have someone of his calibre on the staff full time,' Jenna said regretfully. 'You'll have to get him to recommend one of his colleagues to move down here.'

By the time Jenna had done what she could to familiarise Helen with the layout of the cardiac unit and the operating theatre they would be using, and the two of them had completed their preparatory tasks, Noah had finished his discussions with the surgeon who had invited him down to Cornwall, and it was time to meet his young patients.

'This is Daniel Polruan, and he's just turned two,' Jenna began, reading from his file as the youngster was settled on his mother's knee. He was a lovely youngster, with dark hair and large dark eyes with a serious expression.

'Hello, Mrs Polruan.' Noah offered his hand and a warm smile. 'I'm Mr Kincaid.'

'My husband couldn't come today because 'e's on shift work, but 'e's day off tomorrow so 'e'll be here then.'

'That's good. I can always answer his questions later.'

'You'm the one who's going to be doing the operation, then?'

'That's right.' He sat himself down on the chair beside the young woman, and offered his hand for little Daniel to explore. 'How much do you understand of what's the matter with Daniel's heart?'

'Our doctor said that when 'e was still growing inside the heart worked different because he didn' need to breathe. 'E said that usually the extra vein-thing closes up after baby's born, but Daniel's didn' so his blood is going wrong way and straining 'is heart.' She looked up with a questioning expression. 'Is that right?'

'I couldn't have put it better myself,' Noah said reassuringly. 'It's a condition called patent ductus arteriosus.'

'And you'm going to put it right?'

'I hope so, Mrs Polruan. Tomorrow we'll take Daniel into Theatre. . .' Helen hid a smile as she saw Noah reach for his usual pad of paper and pencil and begin to sketch the outline of a heart. 'We've taken pictures so we know what to expect, but when we get to his heart we'll be able to see this extra link between these two blood vessels and we'll be able to close it off so that the blood won't be fighting to go the wrong way.'

'Does that mean 'e won't be poorly any more?'

'Hopefully, after he gets over the operation, he'll begin to catch up with himself. Once his body gets used to the changes he shouldn't have the feeding difficulties, so he should start putting weight on more normally and he shouldn't have so many chest infections. With any luck, his scar will be the only reminder of the problem that he'll be left with.'

'I hope you'm right, Doctor,' the young woman said fervently, cradling her little boy on her lap. 'Daniel's a happy boy but this 'as been holding 'im back terrible.'

'Well, I promise to do my best, so you keep your fingers crossed for him.'

Jenna escorted Daniel and his mother back to the ward while Helen brought the next family in to meet Noah.

'This is Leah Parsons,' she said as she directed the little girl's parents to make themselves comfortable. 'She's four months old.'

'Hello, Mr and Mrs Parsons,' Noah greeted them warmly, but as soon as they were settled his attention immediately went to the lethargic child, cradled in her mother's arms. 'Hello, sweetheart,' he said softly and Helen felt her heart turn over when she watched him stroke the baby's cheek with one gentle finger.

'She's not getting any better,' Mr Parsons said as he watched his little daughter smile half-heartedly up at Noah. 'She's not gaining weight, and she seems to be so tired all the time.'

'And her face is always that funny colour,' his wife added. 'The midwife called her a blue baby when she was born.'

'I expect you've found out since that's because she hasn't got enough oxygen in her blood,' Noah explained simply, and reached for the ubiquitous pad of paper to start his drawings. 'The condition is called transposition of the great vessels, or TGV. . .'

'So,' Mr Parsons said several minutes later as he summarised the information Noah had given him, 'the two arteries grew in the wrong place so one side of her heart sends blood around her body with no oxygen in it, and the other side keeps sending the same blood to the lungs to pick up more oxygen.'

'Exactly.' Noah nodded. 'And if it wasn't for the fact that Leah's also got a hole between the two sides of the heart to allow the two separate blood circulations to mix she would already be dead.'

'So tomorrow you're going to cut the two arteries and cross them over so they're in the right places, and then mend the hole between the two halves of the heart?'

'That's right.' Noah smiled encouragingly. 'That hole is the only thing keeping her alive at the moment, but after we've repositioned the arteries it will actually be a defect.'

'Rather you than me, Doctor,' Mr Parsons said as he

shook his head at the complexity of the operation. 'I have enough trouble sewing a button on.'

They were all laughing as Jenna arrived to usher the Parsons family back to the ward, and Helen marvelled at the difference a few kind words and some human warmth and patience made.

In her nursing career she'd known more than a few specialists who were far too conscious of their own importance. They'd completely forgotten that patients and their families would cope with the trauma of major surgery a whole lot better if they had confidence—if they weren't scared to death by being kept in the dark about what was going on.

'And who is this pretty girl?'

Noah's teasing voice drew Helen back to the business in hand and she watched him work his charm on the three-year-old girl being carried in by her father.

'This is Kate Trebetherick,' she said with a smile of her own when she saw the matched pair of dimples the youngster had just shown off for Noah.

'Hello, Kate,' he said and offered her his hand. At first she acted coy but soon she was shaking his hand in grave imitation of her parents.

'This is your second turn through the mill,' Noah commented understandingly to Kate's parents.

'Yes. The first time she had to come in she was only six weeks old,' Mrs Trebetherick confirmed. 'I'm just hoping that everything goes well this time so she doesn't have to have any more operations.'

Helen wasn't able to take quite such a detached view of this child's operation as she had with the other two because Kate suffered from tetralogy of Fallot, the same combination of defects as her own son. The complex operation which Noah would be performing, and at which she would be an important associate, was almost exactly the same as the one he would be performing on Nash in less than two weeks.

Even though she had acted as his senior nurse on a couple of cases before and had researched all the possible variations of the condition and its surgical correction, she was still compelled to listen to his careful explanation as he drew his diagrams for the Trebethericks.

'Did you get everything organised to your satisfaction?' Noah enquired when they finally settled themselves into the back of the taxi, which was returning them to the hotel.

'Everything,' Helen confirmed quietly. 'Jenna's obviously very experienced in theatre work. She was working in the hospital for several years before they opened the cardiac unit, so she knows her way around.'

'God, I'm tired.' Noah sighed deeply and leaned his head back against the high seat. 'Sometimes I think dealing with the families is more exhausting than doing the operations.'

'Well, it would be,' Helen replied pertly, watching the way the streetlights outlined his profile and picked up fugitive gleams from his eyes as he watched the passing scenery. 'Unconscious patients don't ask questions and can't talk back!'

'You could have something there. . .' He rolled his head until he was watching her, and Helen wondered what he was thinking.

The feminine side of her wished that she hadn't just flopped herself into a heap in the corner of the seat. In spite of the fact that she'd changed her clothes when they'd reached the hospital, she felt as if she must look like a scruffy bundle of washing. . .

'Do you want to go out for a meal?' he asked, and her heart gave a silly leap at the idea that he was inviting her out. Then she saw how tired he looked and remembered that he had a full day in Theatre tomorrow. . .

'I think I'm too tired to appreciate an evening out,' she said with regret. 'And with the prospect of several long days and late nights until you're happy with their progress. . .'

He sighed heavily.

'I suppose you're right,' he agreed. 'I just thought it might be an idea if we took the opportunity to get to know each other a bit before we have to face an inquisition in Q'ran.'

Helen's heart sank a little when he detailed his reasons for asking her out. For a moment her heart had leapt at the thought that he wanted her company.

'We could always blame our lack of detailed knowledge about each other on the fact that we've only recently married,' she suggested.

'Looks as if we might have to—at this rate, we're not even going to know whether we take sugar in our coffees.'

It sounded almost as if Noah regretted the fact that the two of them had spent so little time together so far—but *he* had been the one to make certain that he never came to bed until she was asleep, and *he* was the one who was always dressed and gone before she was awake. . .

Her thoughts occupied her right up to the moment she stepped inside the suite and caught sight of the open door on the other side of the reception area—the one which led into the bedroom.

Suddenly she remembered how the room was decorated

and had to face the fact that she was going to have to go into that room and sleep in it.

Without being aware of it, she had come to a halt just inside the door—her eyes fixed on the wedge of room visible through the open door with all the awful fascination of someone seeing a deadly snake.

'Helen. . .?'

She hadn't realised how cold her hands were until Noah wrapped them in his own warm ones and held them against his chest.

'Do you want me to ask the hotel to move us to another room?' he offered, moving to position his own body between her and her view of the bedroom.

For just a second she nearly leapt at the idea, but something made her hold her tongue while she thought about the consequences if she did.

When she realised that moving to another room would be tantamount to giving in to Mahmoud's brand of terrorism everything inside her rose up in revolt.

'No. . .' she said in a less than steady voice, then lifted her chin and began again. 'No, thank you, Noah. That won't be necessary. Besides, Peter would be so disappointed after his efforts to surprise us. . .'

'You're certain?' He fixed her with darkly intent eyes, and she could see the questions teeming there.

'Quite certain,' she repeated, and found that suddenly she was.

There was something in his honest concern for her feelings which overrode her fears and somehow she knew that, with Noah beside her, she could cope with the memories.

'In that case,' he said calmly, taking her at her word, 'if you'd like to have a look at the menu for room service and tell me what you'd like, I'll give you first shot at the bathroom while I phone the orders through. Be warned, though—if you're not out of there by the time the food arrives, I'm eating yours too!'

'That was delicious,' Noah said as he left the table. He linked his fingers together and stretched his arms over head to loosen the muscles in his shoulders, then reached for the telephone again. 'Now all you need is. . . Ah!'

Someone had obviously answered the call.

'Could you send up some Armagnac? The name is Kincaid. . . Yes, that's the honeymoon suite. . . Thank you.' He put the phone down rather abruptly, and turned towards Helen with a scowl on his face. 'Couldn't Peter have been satisfied with changing the booking from two single rooms to a double? Why did he have to put us in the honeymoon suite?'

The disgust in his voice, coupled with the heightened colour along his cheek-bones, had Helen biting her tongue to stop the laughter escaping. She would never have thought that someone as self-contained as Noah Kincaid would have been embarrassed like this.

Helen had been surprised to hear him ordering the liqueur, but when the single glass of amber-coloured liquid was delivered she was even more surprised when he presented it to her.

'For me? But. . .'

'I've made it a practice never to drink alcohol or coffee for twelve hours before surgery ever since I realised that it could cause hand tremors,' he said, confirming what she'd already known. 'I ordered the Armagnac for you.' He held the elegant glass towards her. 'I think you'll like it—it's mellower than cognac.'

'But I don't usually drink spirits. I haven't got the head for it,' she objected weakly.

'All the better,' he said with satisfaction in his voice. 'It will help you to sleep, in spite of your surroundings.'

At his cryptic comment, Helen glanced towards the bedroom door and accepted the glass silently.

She was already so tired after the journey down from London that it only took a few sips of the potent alcohol before she was almost falling asleep in the armchair, and Noah took her hand and urged her to her feet.

'We could leave the light on out here to find our way around in the bedroom,' he suggested matter-of-factly. 'I thought that if you couldn't see the details in there too clearly it might make it easier for you to cope. . .' He allowed his words to die away.

'Thank you,' she whispered through a throat grown tight with the threat of tears at the continuing evidence of his thoughtfulness. 'You're a very nice man, aren't you?'

Part of her brain was conscious that the small amount of alcohol had taken the brakes off her tongue. . . After all, she was only telling the truth. She *did* think he was a very nice man. . .and a very good looking one. . .and far too sexy for her peace of mind. . .

She must have been asleep almost before her head hit the pillow because several hours had passed by the time she drifted briefly towards wakefulness.

Even that small amount of alcohol had left her muzzy-headed because suddenly she couldn't remember where she was, and her sudden realisation that there was another person in her bed took on all the characteristics of her worst nightmares.

'No. . .' she whimpered as the shaking began to take possession of her clammy body, and she put her hand

out to push him away. 'Please, Mahmoud. . . No. . . Not
again. . .!'

The figure beside her stirred, and a hand reached out
to switch on the bedside light as he turned towards her
and raised himself up on one elbow.

As her surroundings were flooded with instant light she
was searingly conscious of the figure poised in menacing
silhouette over her and she shrank back against the pillows,
her heart frantically pounding in her throat as she tried to
draw breath into her paralysed lungs.

'No. . .' she moaned, bracing both hands against his
naked chest, her anguish soul-deep as she waited for it to
begin. 'Please. . . Don't do it any more. . . Please. . .!'

'Helen?'

The deep voice barely penetrated her terror and when
he trapped her flailing hands in his much stronger ones
she rolled her head from side to side in blind denial, biting
her lip to prevent the screams which would only earn her
further punishment.

'Helen! Stop it!' The words were a clear command, but
the accent was wrong—it didn't belong in the nightmare
which had plagued her for so long.

'Helen?'

The insistent repetition of her voice finally dragged her
out of the deadly spiral, and she blinked in shock as she
stared up into Noah's face.

# CHAPTER SEVEN

ONCE again Helen was sitting beside Noah in a plane about to come in to land, but this time there was little evidence outside the windows of the comforting green hills of England.

'Are you all right?' Noah murmured as he reached across and twined his fingers with hers. Out of deference to the fact that they couldn't be sure who might be listening to their conversation, they kept their voices low.

The only person they knew on the flight was Peter, and they could be certain that if he noticed them whispering together he would just take it for typical newly-wed behaviour and would probably tease them for it at the first opportunity.

'I'm nervous,' Helen admitted equally softly, knowing that he could feel the fine tremor in her hand. 'Especially now that we're nearly there.'

'Well, we've done everything we can to disguise your original identity. . .' His dark blue gaze skimmed upwards from the blue-tinted lenses she told him she'd worn ever since her recovery from the attempt on her life and settled on the nondescript mid-brown colour she had decided to use to darken the striking blonde of her natural hair.

'I just hope we haven't overlooked anything obvious,' she whispered. 'It matters so much. . .'

He squeezed her hand and smiled down at her, and she marvelled at the change in their relationship in the last ten days.

It all dated back to the time she'd woken up to her living nightmare in the hotel in Cornwall.

He'd been very gentle and very kind, but he'd persisted until he'd persuaded her to tell him what it had all been about.

At his insistence, she'd told him that as soon as Nash's heart condition had been diagnosed—and its significance had been explained to Mahmoud—her ex-husband had cruelly insisted that she should become pregnant again as soon as possible to provide him with a 'perfect' son in place of the flawed one she had produced. He'd declared that he had too much at stake to risk everything on an heir with a diseased heart, and that it was Helen's duty to submit to his wishes.

By this time, she'd had months of isolation and loneliness in which to realise that the man she had married in such high hopes didn't really exist and that, without even the pretence of love between them, she couldn't face the intimacy he wanted.

*That* had been when she'd finally realised that Mahmoud had cared nothing at all for her because when she'd tried to explain her feelings, in the hope that he'd let her go, he'd just laughed at her.

When she'd sobbed out her heartbreak at Mahmoud's repeated rapes on Noah's comforting shoulder Helen had heard his tight-lipped curses, and at last had known that someone really cared for her.

She'd fallen asleep in his arms that night, her head pillowed close to the steady beat of his heart and, even on their return to St Augustine's, the same thing had happened every night since.

Helen glanced across at his concerned expression as the plane circled for the final approach and returned the pressure of his hand, welcoming the growing closeness between them and confident that she could trust Noah to help her through the coming confrontation.

'Welcome to Q'ran,' the white-robed young man said with a bow as soon as they escaped the searing heat of the runway and entered the air-conditioned airport building. 'It is an honour that you have come to our country.'

'We are honoured to have been invited,' Noah returned politely in his role as leader of the team.

Obviously the young man's position was well known because they were all whisked smartly through customs with barely a glance at their precious passports and other paperwork.

'Relax. Stage three successfully completed,' Noah murmured supportively to Helen under cover of the rapid chattering as their personal and medical luggage was piled into a small fleet of gleaming limousines by a group of uniformed Q'rani airport employees.

'At least we'll be able to unwind a little when we get to our rooms,' she replied, not certain whether she was voicing her thoughts for his benefit or her own.

All she knew was that she hadn't been in Q'ran for an hour and already she was longing to arrive safely at their hotel. She needed to be able to go somewhere where she wouldn't be aware that the people watching her and listening to what she was saying could be in Mahmoud's employ and only too willing to report any inadvertent slip back to him.

'If you would please to get in the cars now,' the young emissary of their hosts asked with yet another bow. 'Ahmad bin Ali has requested that you will honour him by staying in his home while you are in our country.'

Helen's hand tightened like a vice around Noah's arm, and she couldn't prevent the moan of despair which escaped her as she heard the words.

'But we couldn't possibly impose on Ahmad bin Ali's generosity in such a way,' he began politely, his hand tightening supportively. 'Especially when we are already booked in to one of Q'ran's best and most modern hotels.'

'Ahmad bin Ali has asked me to inform you that he has taken the liberty of cancelling your reservations at the hotel so that you might sample the true hospitality of our country.'

For Helen the combination of stress and heat, compounded with the shocking news that they were expected to stay in the one place in the whole of Q'ran which was the focus of all her unhappiness, was enough to take the starch out of her knees.

As the waves of heat rose up from the broad expanse of concrete to surround her she found it increasingly hard to focus on the conversation going on above her head and, in spite of her best efforts, a strange darkness pressed in on her and she felt herself begin to slide out of Noah's grasp towards the ground. . .

'Helen. . .'

She heard the voice calling her, but it was too pleasant floating in the cool darkness to pay much attention.

'Come on, Helen. . . Wake up. . .'

The voice was trying to intrude again and it was getting harder to ignore.

'Open your eyes, sweetheart. . .'

It was the worried tone in the deep husky voice which finally persuaded her to make the effort, and she lifted heavy lids to look up into Noah's dark blue eyes.

'Helen,' he breathed softly, relief evident on his face

as well as in his voice. 'Are you feeling better?' He stroked his hand over her forehead, smoothing away the tendrils of hair plastered there by perspiration in spite of the fact that they were now cocooned in the air-conditioned car.

'Too hot,' she whispered while she tried to remember what had happened. 'Couldn't breathe. . . Oh!' Suddenly she *did* remember what had caused the sensory overload which had made her faint.

'Oh, Noah!' she wailed softly as she turned her head into his shoulder, afraid that their driver might be able to understand English. 'We're not really going to Ahmad bin Ali's, are we?'

'I'm afraid so,' he admitted, sparing a brief glance towards the impassive figure behind the wheel before he spoke directly into her ear. 'There really wasn't any polite way to get out of it.'

Helen moaned her distress and shook her head.

'Helen, who *is* he?' Noah demanded huskily. 'Someone important? Someone who knows your ex-husband and might recognise you?'

'He's Mahmoud's uncle,' she said in a voice that wobbled in spite of her best efforts. 'It was *his* house I lived in when I was married to Mahmoud.'

'So. . . We're going back to the same house?'

Helen nodded as the bitter irony struck her again.

'There's no chance now,' she muttered to herself, her voice muffled against his chest as she faced the ruination of her most cherished dreams. 'If it had been anywhere else I could have found a way, but not in that house. . .'

'Shh, Helen. Don't get yourself upset,' Noah murmured as he cradled her head against his shoulder with one hand. 'I'm sure it will all work out in the end. It might even work out better if we're living in the same house—you might have an even greater chance to spend time with Nash.'

But no chance at all to rescue him and take him back to England, she thought despairingly, her heart clenching tightly with pain when she realised that this was the one dream that she hadn't dared confide to Noah.

'Welcome. Welcome.'

They'd drawn up outside the front of the all-too-familiar, sprawling, white-painted house, and the door of the car had hardly had time to open before Helen could hear the accented voice greeting them.

With a sinking heart she became aware that she recognised the courtly tones, and realised that Ahmad bin Ali had come to welcome them personally.

'Prepare for stage four,' Noah muttered with a final squeeze of his arm around her shoulders before he turned to climb out of the car and into the debilitating heat.

Noah's deliberate use of the catch phrase they'd begun to resort to when they discussed the possible points of danger was enough to have her straightening her shoulders and lifting her chin, ready to do battle.

If she was to collapse now it wouldn't just be herself she was letting down but the whole team, and there was no way she was going to do that.

She followed Noah out of the same side of the car, moving discreetly so that she didn't draw any undue attention to herself. Quietly she went and stood beside him, deliberately positioning herself so that she was partly in his shadow.

She could have laughed at the irony which told her that Ahmad bin Ali would thoroughly approve of the modest way she was behaving in the presence of men other than her husband.

When she'd first come to this house, believing that she was Mahmoud's much-loved wife, she'd soon discovered that his powerful and obscenely wealthy uncle, Ahmad, was a very old-fashioned man who still believed that a husband had the absolute right to order every minute of his wife's life if he wished. He had never understood or accepted the fact that Helen—or Eleanor, as she'd been then—might have had ideas of her own, or that she might expect to join in a conversation as a man's equal.

'We are honoured that you have invited us to stay in your home,' Noah said formally.

'The honour is mine,' their host replied. 'It is but a small thing when you have come to spend time in our hospital with our sick children. Please. . .' He gestured for them to precede him through the heavy wooden doors, standing open in the thick white wall, and into the shadowy interior. 'Welcome to my home,' he reiterated.

It wasn't until Helen heard the hiss of amazement behind her that she remembered that Peter had followed them into the house.

They had all paused just inside the door while their eyes became accustomed to the change in light, and found themselves in the ideal position to look through an archway on the other side of the entrance hall and into an enclosed courtyard, full of the sound of splashing water and an absolute riot of colour from the profusion of flowers.

'Wait,' Helen whispered, hanging onto Noah's elbow when he would have walked forward to view the enticing scene. 'Shoes,' she hissed in a timely reminder, and nudged him towards the row of slippers against the wall beside the front door, toeing off her own shoes and sliding her feet into the replacements provided.

'Well done,' Peter murmured as he followed suit. 'I'd forgotten about this custom. Wouldn't want to get up the nose of the local bigwigs.'

Peter's typical irreverence was just the leaven her spirits needed, and there was a new lightness in her step as she followed the two men towards the place which had been her favourite when she'd lived here before.

'This is wonderful,' Peter said enthusiastically as he looked around at the brilliant blooms, tumbling over every size and shape of pot and clambering up walls and over arches. 'I've never seen anywhere so beautiful.'

'Thank you.' Ahmad inclined his head graciously, as though the whole display was his own unaided work. Helen hid a wry smile, knowing that he'd never seen the point of dirtying his hands when he could pay someone to do the job for him.

'If you would like to wait here for a minute I will send someone to show you to your rooms, but please feel free to return here whenever you wish.'

Helen gave a sigh of relief when the old tyrant finally disappeared through an archway on the other side of the small fountain set in the centre of the courtyard, and she stepped forward to dabble her fingers in the cool water.

'You wouldn't know this was here at all,' Peter said, still enraptured by the unexpected delight. 'From the outside the house just looked like a boring square block.'

'They're built to face inward because this style of construction provides somewhere safe for the family, and also somewhere cool to withstand the incredible heat and dryness.'

'You're not kidding about the heat,' Peter commented, his freckled face quite red. 'We left a typical English summer day and stepped off the plane into an open furnace. I'm not dressed right for this.'

'Well, don't make the mistake of stripping off,' Noah warned. 'Your skin would burn in about ten minutes in this sun, and you'd be blistered in twenty.'

'There's no way I'm keeping all these clothes on,' he objected, obviously uncomfortable.

'Wear a loose long-sleeved shirt—I did warn you to make sure as many of your clothes were cotton as possible,' Noah advised.

'You'll probably find that there's a cotton robe provided in your room,' Helen suggested quietly. 'Something a bit like a kaftan. . .' She bit her lip when she suddenly realised that she might be saying too much. If one of the servants, or even one of the family, was listening they might wonder how a stranger knew such things. . .

'You mean, a bit like the towelling robes some of the big hotels provide for their guests?'

Helen nodded silently, not wanting to commit herself any further, but Peter hardly noticed her reticence.

'Well, Noah, are you game to walk around in one too?' Pete challenged.

'Why not?' Noah replied calmly. 'As the saying goes, "when in Rome. . ."'

The soft slap of slippers on the cool marble floor alerted all three of them that someone was coming, and Helen was shocked to recognise the stunningly beautiful young woman who entered the courtyard.

'My name is Nour.' She introduced herself with an open smile, her eyes as dark and lustrous as her long hair. 'If you would like to follow me, I'll show you to your rooms.'

'Anywhere. . .' Peter muttered under his breath with a

bemused expression on his face. 'I'll follow you anywhere you ask. . .'

'Careful, Peter,' Helen warned with a surreptitious dig in his ribs to catch his attention. 'You're going to trip over your tongue. . .'

She heard Noah's quiet snort as she followed him out of the courtyard, but she didn't feel quite so much like laughing when she realised the direction in which they were going.

On the pretext of admiring the intricacies of the inlaid pattern of tiles, she managed to prolong their journey until she thought she'd regained her composure. When Nour opened the heavy wooden door to show Noah and herself into the room they'd been given she'd prepared herself for the idea of spending the next few nights in the room which had once been her own.

What she wasn't prepared for was the shock of finding out that the room had been left exactly as she had designed it, with every piece of furniture she'd chosen exactly where she had placed it and her colour scheme intact.

'Dear God,' she whispered as she sank down on the edge of the bed and gazed around herself in a mixture of horror and amazement, her eyes eventually alighting on Noah as he watched her strange reaction to the room.

'What's the matter, Helen?' he asked with a puzzled frown pleating his forehead and drawing his dark blond eyebrows together. 'Is it something to do with the room. . .?'

He paused when he saw her shake her head emphatically, her finger at her lips in the age-old gesture for silence.

'I wonder where the bathroom is?' she said in an over-bright voice, and beckoned for him to follow her as she led the way into the *en suite* bathroom.

There, too, everything was as she remembered, and an uncomfortable shiver spasmed its way down her spine.

'This is nice,' she said clearly, keeping up the performance. 'I can't wait to have a cool shower. . .' She reached into the modern shower enclosure and twisted the controls until the water started gushing out then adjusted the shower head until the water began to play against the surround, making a sound just like a hailstorm.

'What on *earth* is going on, Helen? Are you sure you're feeling. . .?'

'I'm sorry about all the cloak-and-dagger nonsense, Noah, but it's this room. . .' She gestured with one hand to include the bedroom. 'This was my suite when I was pregnant with Nash. Mahmoud let me decorate it how I wanted and. . . It's as if I've never been away—as if the last two years haven't existed. . .'

'You mean everything's been left as it was?'

'Everything.'

'But that doesn't explain the high jinks with the shower. What's the point of that?'

'I didn't realise it for a long time, but the arrangement of the rooms at this end of the house means that anyone sitting in a certain place in the courtyard can hear everything that goes on in here. It was Mahmoud's way of keeping an eye on me—until Nour let me in on the secret.'

A dull thudding sound came from the direction of the bedroom, and they both turned to look in that direction.

'Hey, you two! No time for naughty stuff!' Peter's voice called as Noah reached in to turn the shower off. 'Nour said she was going to get some drinks ready for us. I'll see you in the courtyard.'

There was one final thump before they heard his footsteps, receding down the corridor.

'What would we ever do without Pete?' Noah said wryly, then pulled an appreciative face when he opened the beautifully carved wardrobe to find that all their clothes had already been hung up.

'He certainly sounds much happier about the heat since he met Nour,' Helen commented with a grin.

'Is he likely to cause a problem if he sets off in hot pursuit of her?' Noah asked softly, bearing in mind the fact that their conversation was no longer being covered by the sound of the shower.

'Nour is very good at taking care of herself,' Helen confirmed with a reminiscent smile. 'You'll see. . .'

By the time Noah and Helen left their room to join Peter again they could hear from the number of voices that there was a general gathering of the family taking place in the courtyard.

Helen faltered for a second as they reached the archway and she caught her first glimpse of the dark-haired man who had once promised to love her for ever.

'Mahmoud?' Noah questioned in a soft murmur, and Helen answered with a silent nod. 'He wasn't nearly good enough for you,' Noah said outrageously. 'Not tall enough, and definitely not good-looking enough.'

There was more than a trace of impish laughter on her face as Helen looked up at Noah. 'Not blond enough?' she prompted wickedly.

'Not nearly blond enough,' he agreed, and they were both laughing at their nonsensical conversation when they stepped out to join the rest of the group.

'Ah. Here is the good doctor now,' Ahmad announced. 'Will you let me introduce my family to you?'

Noah shook hands with Mahmoud when they were introduced and, when it looked as if he would completely ignore Helen, returned the compliment by introducing her as an important member of the team and also his wife.

Noah managed to imbue the word with so much pride that Helen was touched, the feared introduction becoming so meaningless that she hardly noticed the obligatory bow her ex-husband performed.

The introductions over, everyone went to sit themselves down with a long refreshing drink. Helen suddenly caught sight of the silent member of the party who had been hidden behind Mahmoud until now.

For a second she froze—the way a wild animal did when in the presence of a perceived danger. Her tension must have communicated itself to Noah because he chose that precise moment to lean towards her and break the spell.

'Do I take it that the life and soul of the party is wife number one?' he murmured surreptitiously, and she couldn't help smiling, mentally blessing him for coming to her rescue yet again as she managed to meet the flat animosity of her old enemy's gaze.

'I understand that there will be an extra patient for us to see tomorrow,' Noah commented when the pleasantries had died away. 'The hospital director said it is due to your generosity, sir.' He bowed slightly in Ahmad's direction.

'Ah. It is nothing,' he said with a dismissive wave of his hand. 'The child has the same condition as Nashir's, and if you have enough time to stay the extra days you are welcome to spend them in my house. As for the hospital, the director has assured me that there would be enough room in the unit for the extra child to be taken care of. . .'

Ahmad shrugged, as if the topic was unimportant, but Helen's curiosity was aroused. When she had the first faint glimmerings of an idea to solve her problem she wondered how she could go about finding out more about this other child, without raising anyone's suspicions.

'I presume all the relevant diagnostic tests have been done?' Noah asked with understandable concern.

'Of course,' a female voice replied, and Helen was surprised to realise that it was Nour who had spoken. 'He had a Blalock-Taussig shunt done about two years ago,' she continued, obviously knowing exactly what she was talking about. 'But he's ready now for total correction and the removal of the shunt.'

'We'll have to go over all his results, of course,' Noah cautioned. 'But, if everything is right, there's no reason why we shouldn't have plenty of time to fit him in.'

'Good.' Nour gave him a beaming smile, her teeth very white against her smooth, olive-toned skin. 'I'll make certain everything is ready for you when you come to the hospital in the morning.'

'Nour's your opposite number here, Helen,' Peter announced as proudly as if he were responsible for her promotion himself, and confirmed Helen's growing suspicion.

The first time she'd met Nour she'd been struck by the young woman's dedication. It was wonderful to come back and find out that her determination to train for paediatric nursing had been fulfilled.

'And the original patient?' Helen dared to ask, her voice husky with tension that the question might draw undue attention to her.

'My nephew, Nashir,' Nour explained. 'My sister,

Fatima, has been taking care of her him while he waits for his operation.'

This was not the news that Helen had wanted to hear. She knew of old that Fatima resented Nash's very existence. . .

'Is he in the house, or has he already gone to the hospital?' Noah enquired, realising that Helen was desperate to know.

'Oh, he's still here,' Nour said brightly. 'He's not due to go in until tomorrow morning. I'm going to take him in with me when I go on duty. Would you like to meet him?'

Helen wanted to leap out of her seat and shout out her eagerness but she sat still and waited for Noah's quiet agreement, only then standing up on legs trembling with eagerness to follow Nour as she led them through to the opposite side of the house.

Nash's room was the same one which she had chosen and decorated while she still believed that her marriage had a chance of success, but the cheerful decorations and bright furnishings she'd lovingly assembled had all disappeared.

The thin, solemn child propped up at forty-five degrees to assist his breathing wasn't the same bright, alert child she'd last seen, and Helen could have wept.

'Hello, Nashir,' Nour greeted him as she led them into the room, and Helen was so busy filling her eyes with every detail of his appearance that it took several seconds before she realised that she'd done so in English.

'He speaks English?' She pounced on the evidence eagerly, desperately hoping that one of the hurdles between them had ceased to exist.

'Only a few words,' Nour admitted apologetically. 'I've tried to keep it up for him, in honour of his mother, but my sister objects. . .' She shrugged expressively. 'Fatima is not a happy woman,' she added almost under her breath.

'Is he nervous of strangers?' Helen asked, forcing herself to hold back when all she wanted to do was go to him and gather him up in her arms.

'Not particularly, because he's had so many looking after him but he's too. . .' she seemed to be casting about for the word she wanted '. . .passive is the word, I think. He doesn't seem to mind who does things for him, but it's as if he won't let himself become attached to anyone.'

Tears were trying to force their way up, but Helen wouldn't allow it as she approached her son for the first time in over two years.

'Hello,' she said quietly as she knelt down beside his chair, then paused as the dark eyes she remembered so well looked her over with a seriousness beyond his years. 'Would you like me to read you a story?' she offered impulsively, almost desperate to make some kind of contact with him as she reached for a discarded book.

For a long time he was silent, and she wasn't certain whether he'd understood her question or even if he was interested in her offer.

Just when she was beginning to give up hope she saw a spark of curiosity brighten his eyes.

'Yes,' he whispered finally. 'Please. . .'

# CHAPTER EIGHT

'OH, NOAH,' Helen wept as he cradled her in his arms in the bathroom.

Once again the shower was running to cover their conversation, but it was Noah who'd had to remember to set up the ploy. Helen had been beyond rational thought by the time they'd returned to their room.

'What have they done to my happy baby?' she sobbed. 'He's such an unhappy little boy now.'

'He's been ill for a long time,' Noah reminded her softly as he stroked her hair away from her hot face. 'You know as well as I do that children with his cardiac problems don't have much energy to spare, even with a shunt.'

'But they've killed his spirit,' she spat fiercely, glaring at him out of tear-filled eyes almost as if she was blaming him for what had happened.

Her explosion into anger and tears was long overdue. She'd managed to contain her emotions throughout an interminable meal when they'd all been forced to obey the rules of politeness.

Under her slightly distant smiles, as she'd responded to the flow of social chit-chat, she'd been filled with pain and sorrow for the sad little shadow Nash had become.

She'd barely managed to subdue her need to lash out at the people who had made him that way, charitably putting it down to indifference rather than deliberate neglect or cruelty—for the sake of her own sanity.

In the end, the only things which had helped her to hold

her tongue were the thought that she mustn't do anything to jeopardise her chance of rescuing him and the sweet memory of the way he had allowed her to lift him on her lap while she read him first one story and then a second.

She'd relished the way he'd accepted her encircling arm as she'd pointed out the simple words on the page, grateful all over again that she'd made the effort to get that far with her Arabic studies.

She'd barely noticed Nour's speculative looks as she'd wordlessly produced a rather tattered story-book written in English, then waited beside an equally silent Noah while Helen told the familiar tales to her enthralled little audience of one.

Too soon it had been time to leave him and join the rest of the family for the torture of a formal meal but at least she'd left Nash knowing that, for the first time since he'd been so brutally stolen from her, she'd been the one to settle her frail son down to sleep.

'They haven't really killed his spirit,' Noah insisted in a voice of utter conviction. 'Not if he's really your son.'

He cupped her cheek in his hand and tilted her face up until she was forced to meet his dark blue gaze. 'He might have been flattened temporarily by the force of circumstances, but there's no way anyone could have killed his spirit if he inherited it from you.'

His arms were wrapped tightly around her as they stood in the incongruous surroundings of the luxurious bathroom, and he rocked her as if she were no more than a child herself.

Slowly the storm of tears abated and she was left feeling utterly drained, grateful for the untiring support of Noah's strong arms.

'I'm sorry,' she whispered, feeling more exhausted than

she'd ever been before. 'It wasn't fair of me to take it all out on you. . .'

'Shh,' Noah soothed. 'I've got broad enough shoulders to cope with it.' He cradled her head back down against him. 'Just catch your breath for a minute,' he advised.

Gradually Helen became aware of her surroundings again, and her ears focused on the background noise of the water droplets striking the shower enclosure. Suddenly the incongruity of the situation struck her and she began to giggle.

'You'll give me a complex if you're laughing at my shoulders,' Noah warned.

'No. Never,' she said fervently. 'It's just. . . Anyone listening outside is going to wonder what on earth we're doing with the shower running so long. They'll think we've got some sort of water fetish. . .'

She looked up at Noah, expecting him to join her laughter, but the fleeting expression she surprised in his eyes drove all thought of levity out of her head.

She'd never seen such heat and hunger in his eyes, but before she could be certain that her own eyes weren't mistaken he'd dropped his usual internal shutters and he was the same calm man she'd always known.

Except. . .

'Noah. . .?' she began tentatively, then had to stop because she didn't know how to continue; didn't know if she was making an embarrassing mistake. . .

'You must be exhausted,' Noah broke in prosaically as he leant across to turn off the shower. 'I think it's time you caught up on your sleep. . .'

'Noah?'

Helen put her hand on his sleeve to stop him turning the control, and was suddenly aware of the warmth and strength of the lean muscles hidden under the plain white cotton sleeve of his shirt.

'What?' he asked, his voice strangely husky.

As soon as she'd touched him he'd frozen, his dark eyes intent as he looked down at her.

'I. . .' She bit her lip and glanced away, looking at anything rather than the man in front of her while she tried to find the courage and the words.

'I—I need a shower,' she said in a rush, then huffed out an exasperated breath when he took a step back from her.

'I'll leave you to it, then,' he offered and went to go around her.

'No. . . I. . . Oh, Noah will you stay with me?' she asked, then cringed inwardly at the baldness of the request.

'Of course I will,' he said kindly, and turned to grab a pile of thick towels to place them beside the shower. 'I don't mind staying if you don't want to be alone.'

She could have wept again when she realised that he'd completely misunderstood her intention. She'd thought she'd caught sight of something in his eyes which mirrored the way she was coming to feel about him, but fear that she'd been mistaken held her back from making any more overt advances.

'Can you undo my zip?' She turned her back towards him, falling back on the oldest ploy since zips were invented.

Neither of them moved for a second, and he was so quiet that she almost thought that he was going to refuse her request. Then she felt his fingers at the back of her neck, and a delicious shiver ran the whole length of her spine.

'Thank you,' she murmured when the soft hiss stopped and the soft cotton fabric parted and slid forward over her shoulders. With a single shrug, it pooled around her waist and she freed each arm in turn before the whole dress slithered to the floor and she stepped out of it.

The little voice of her conscience was screaming at her that she shouldn't be doing this. It wasn't fair to Noah— not after all his unselfish support and consideration.

Goose bumps tightened her skin, and her nipples hardened into tight buds at the thought that Noah was watching her undress; that he was standing right behind her while she stood there in her plainest white cotton bra and panties and reached for the hook at the back.

She could have cursed when she realised that her hands were shaking too much to manage the simple task she'd been performing for years but she continued to fumble, knowing that she couldn't just step in under the shower wearing her bra.

'Allow me,' Noah offered, his voice sounding deeper and huskier than ever.

Helen's hands fell bonelessly to her sides as she felt the warmth of his fingers in the middle of her back. There was a soft click as the catch parted, and then he was smoothing the narrow straps over her shoulders and down her arms.

Mesmerised by the unexpected turn of events, she stood silently while he hooked gentle fingers in the narrow elastic encircling her hips and slid her panties down to her knees. Like an automaton, she lifted one foot to free it from her last garment and the plain white cotton fell to the floor to join the rest of her clothes.

'Do you. . .?' He paused to clear his throat but when he began again his voice was still gravelly. 'Will you need me to wash your back?'

Helen could barely breathe, let alone speak, and had

to resort to a silent nod as she stepped into the shower enclosure.

Once she was surrounded by the sound of the water she couldn't hear anything else in the room. She could have turned round to see what Noah was doing, but she seemed to have used up her store of courage for the day and just stared at the tiled wall of the enclosure.

The waft of cool air was the only warning she had that she was no longer alone before two arms wrapped around her from behind and she was pulled back against Noah's naked body.

'Oh, God, you feel good!' he groaned in her ear as he plastered his body so tightly against hers that there was no room even for water between them. 'I hope this was what you wanted because I don't think I can let you go now.'

Helen closed her eyes and leant back against him, revelling in his size and strength as he supported her weight effortlessly.

Her head dropped back onto his shoulder, her face tilted up to the spray with the same innocent pleasure of a child enjoying a summer shower.

'Ah, Helen,' he breathed as he nuzzled the exposed length of her throat. 'I want to touch you all over. . .'

She felt his arms tighten around her and his open hands span her ribs, his fingertips finding the delicate hollows between them as she reached out one hand and felt around blindly.

'Here,' she murmured as her own fingers closed around the soap left ready in the little alcove and she offered him the slippery tablet.

'Are you trying to kill me?' he demanded as he began

by swirling the smooth oval around in circles over the tender skin of her stomach.

'No...but I think I'd die if you stopped what you're doing to me...' She couldn't speak any more, her breathing stopped abruptly by the way his hands had joined in the torment and had slid up to cradle the pouting globes of her breasts.

After that, time seemed to have no meaning as he slowly fulfilled his wish, repeatedly covering his hands with fresh lather—only to smooth it over another area of her body until her nerves were so sensitive that she thought she would scream.

Then his fingers delved between her thighs and she *did* scream, the helpless sound swallowed up in his mouth as he took her to the pinnacle of pleasure for the first time in her life.

She was sobbing again as she spiralled down from unimaginable heights, standing passively as he rinsed the last of the soap from her body and wrapped her in a towel before scooping her up in his arms and carrying her through to the bedroom.

'Oh, Noah, I'm sorry...' she wailed, covering her face with both hands in a mixture of dismay and embarrassment.

'Well, I'm not,' he said firmly as he grasped her wrists and gently pulled her hands away. 'I'm not in the least bit sorry,' he reiterated as he smoothed the wet, tangled strands of hair away from her forehead and deposited a kiss there instead.

She murmured wordlessly and tried to hold onto the towel when he unwound it from her body, shyness suddenly returning with a vengeance, but he wouldn't allow it.

Calmly and steadily he blotted the drops of water from

her skin, then pulled the covers back and helped her to slide between smooth dry cotton sheets.

She felt her eyes grow enormous as she watched him straighten up and unselfconsciously use the same towel to dry the excess moisture off his own body before he wadded it up and aimed it at the bathroom door.

She was still mesmerised by her first view of his naked body when he turned back towards the bed.

'Move over,' he ordered gruffly as he lifted the edge of the sheet and slid in beside her, wrapping his arms around her and pulling her towards him before she could escape to the other side of the bed.

'How could I possibly be sorry?' he demanded huskily as he settled her head on his shoulder. 'In the middle of all the turmoil in your life you trusted me enough to put yourself in my hands. Having told me what Mahmoud put you through, how could you *not* realise what an honour it is?'

'But, I didn't. . . You haven't. . .' She bit her lip in vexation, not knowing how to broach the topic she needed to raise, then moved her thigh almost unconsciously against the evidence of his arousal pressed firmly between them.

'That doesn't matter,' he said calmly as he used one fingertip to trace the smooth curve of each eyebrow.

'But. . .' She tried again.

'It doesn't matter,' he repeated, cradling her cheek in one palm. '*This* is what matters.' He tightened his arm around her shoulders, the action pressing the two of them together from head to toe as he stroked his other hand over her shoulder and down to her hip. 'Closeness matters every bit as much as passion,' he said, his voice a deep rumble in her ear where it was pressed against his chest, and she finally allowed herself to relax.

'The last few weeks have been difficult,' he continued in a soothing murmur. 'Each time I've gone to bed with you I've wanted to take you in my arms; to hold you close and keep you safe. But it wasn't in our arrangement, and I didn't want you to think that I was taking advantage of the situation. . . So I stayed away, knowing that the less time I spent in your company the less chance I had of losing control. . .'

Gradually, as she drifted into sleep, his husky voice faded away entirely but the words lingered in her mind and heart like the sweetest of lullabies.


'Right,' Noah began, all efficiency as he ran through the file detailing young Youssef's results. 'It's obviously another classic case, just like Nashir's.'

'The same single second heart sound for the aortic component, and in the second and third interspaces to the left of the sternum we picked up the same systolic ejection murmur,' Helen supplied, checking the notes she'd taken when she'd listened through the stethoscope. 'The left side of his chest is more prominent, too.'

'These are his latest X-rays,' Peter volunteered as he slid them into position on the viewing box. 'Heart size is normal, as you'd expect, but—in spite of the shunt—the pulmonary segment is still smaller than it should be, and concave—the dye has shown up the great vessels beautifully.'

'What's his blood like?' Noah enquired as he stared at the plates over Peter's shoulder.

'His red cell volume is increased.'

'So? Is it yes or no?' Helen demanded, surreptitiously crossing her fingers. Youssef was so much like Nash that it would break her own heart if he didn't have the same chance at a normal life that Noah would be giving her own son.

'I'd say a definite yes,' Peter said, then looked across at Noah, knowing that the final decision rested in his hands. 'What about you?'

'Unanimous,' Noah agreed with a secret grin for Helen, as if he knew that she'd been willing him to say it.

Helen smiled wholeheartedly back at him, glad that they'd managed to return to their former ease with each other.

When they'd first woken this morning she'd been afraid that her impulsive action last night had ruined everything between them, but when she'd tried to scramble out of bed he'd prevented it by the simple expedient of throwing one leg over hers and wrapping an insistent arm around her shoulders.

'And where do you think *you're* off to?' he'd murmured huskily as he'd settled her more comfortably against him.

'I. . . To the bathroom. . .' she'd begun, stopping when she'd heard how squeaky her voice sounded.

'Don't mention bathrooms,' he'd groaned theatrically and had flung himself back against the pillows. 'Terrible things happen in bathrooms. Wanton women lurk in bathrooms and, when an unsuspecting man wanders by, they insist that you help them out of their clothes and wash them all over.'

'Idiot!' Helen had said with a helpless giggle, her heart suddenly as light and carefree as a helium-filled balloon. 'I suppose you don't accept any of the blame for making free with my poor tired body until I didn't even have the strength to walk through to the bedroom? That was all my fault too?'

'Of course,' he'd said promptly as he'd levered himself up onto one elbow and looked down at her.

With the most innocent of expressions on his face, he slipped the edge of the sheet out of her hand and began to inch it purposefully down towards the tightening evidence of her arousal. 'If the woman lurking in the bathroom possesses the body of a siren she can only blame herself if she ends up utterly exhausted. . .' His voice died away as he finally exposed the deep rosy crests of her nipples and his hand hovered over them.

There was a stealthy noise outside their room which killed their mutual smiles instantly, freezing Noah's fingers in the act of touching her.

'Someone listening?' Noah mouthed and raised an eyebrow.

Helen nodded silently, her heart sinking as the outside world intruded on the light-hearted banter which had accompanied her swift arousal.

'Good morning, sweetheart,' Noah said brightly, his voice slightly louder than normal as he gestured towards the listening ears. 'I hope you slept well last night.'

Helen gasped as he leant forward to press a kiss onto the burgeoning rosy bud, flicking it with his tongue then blowing softly on the wetness he left behind.

'Ah. . . No. . .' she groaned when he leant across her and repeated the gesture on her other breast, leaving both nipples throbbing for his attention.

'I'm sorry you didn't sleep well,' he continued gruffly as his games had a predictable effect on his own body. 'Perhaps I can do something about that for you. . .' His head came down again and Helen watched as he opened his lips just far enough to admit her nipple to the wet warmth inside.

For several seconds he played with her gently and she was just relaxing into the pleasurable sensations in her breast when he began to suckle her, drawing her through the torment of his teeth until she was deep inside his mouth.

Instantly there was a sharp twist of arousal deep inside her, which turned her bones to honey, and her trembling hands came up to cradle his head against her like a precious child, her fingers spearing through the thick silk of his hair.

Suddenly he grew still then dragged his mouth away from her, his hair sliding through her fingers until she was left empty-handed.

'God, I'm sorry,' he groaned and rolled away from her, leaving her feeling utterly bereft. 'I shouldn't have done that,' he said with disgust in his voice.

His words were like a blow and for a moment, as Helen curled herself into a protective ball around her pain, she wondered if the impact would make her sick.

'Can you forgive me?' he murmured in a pained voice.

'What for?' she mumbled flatly, blinking furiously at the gathering tears and determined that she wouldn't allow a single one to fall.

'For starting something we haven't got time to finish,' he said—as though the answer should be obvious—and she felt him roll towards her again, his hand taking hold of her shoulder to turn her to face him.

'Oh, God!' The stricken expression on his face was evidence enough of his contrition when he recognised her hurt. 'Sweetheart, you can't possibly think that I meant. . .' He stopped and pulled a face full of the disgust which had filled his voice before. 'Of course you did,' he murmured, and leant forward to capture her lips in a gentle kiss of contrition.

'Please accept that kiss as an apology and a declaration of intent,' he murmured huskily.

He had cupped one palm around the side of her face to make certain that she was watching him, and she could feel the fine tremor in his hand which told her how seriously he was taking the encounter.

'Intent?' she repeated in a whisper as the fragile flower of hope started to unfurl towards the light.

'Yes. Intent. As in I have every intention of taking up from where we left off this morning and finishing the job properly—just as soon as we get back to this bedroom again!'

Now Helen looked across at Noah with an answering smile, and the happiness she felt was a fine amalgam of her delight that he was going to be operating on Youssef mixed with the heady promise of the pleasures they would share once they returned to Ahmad bin Ali's house.

'Hey, you two—less of the moonstruck expressions, please,' Peter demanded cheekily. 'Honestly, you seem to get worse, not better. . .' he grumbled as he left them in front of the viewing boxes.

Helen felt the instant flood of heat over her cheeks, and chanced a glance at Noah to see how he was taking Peter's comment. She was fascinated to discover that he looked nearly as embarrassed as she did.

'Wretched man,' Noah grumbled as he began to slide all the X-rays and papers back into Youssef's file. 'It's obviously time I sacked him and got someone who knows when to keep quiet. . .'

Helen waited for him to look at her, and they shared another smile.

'And you'd better keep well away from me,' he murmured softly as he began to stalk her on silent feet. 'I don't know exactly how much self-control I've got left, so be warned. . .'

Helen chuckled and flipped him a saucy wave as she whirled and set off in search of Nour.

'They're going to include Youssef,' she announced as soon as she tracked down the beautiful young woman to her own small domain, and they both celebrated the good news.

'This doesn't look much different from my own office,' Helen commented as she saw the pile of patient records Nour was painstakingly updating.

'Just thank goodness that it's not the most important part of the job,' Nour replied. 'You're the same as I am,' she added confidently with an uncomfortably direct look at Helen. 'We can put up with this part for the chance to help the little ones to a new life.'

Helen agreed wholeheartedly, even as she avoided meeting Nour's gaze. An ache of sadness filled her that she couldn't talk to this bright young woman the way she would like to.

They had begun to form a friendship when she had been expecting Nash, the bond all the stronger for their shared interest in nursing in spite of the fact that Nour was Fatima's younger sister and frequently became caught in the middle of the war caused by her sister's hatred for Helen.

Now she didn't dare get too close to her in case she gave too much of herself away. If Nour recognised her she wasn't certain if the young woman would feel obliged to reveal her secret to her family—with catastrophic consequences.

'Eleanor?' Nour said softly, and Helen froze for

a minute before she looked warily across at her.

'I'm sorry. . .' she began, her voice shaking with the force of the sudden pounding of her heart. 'I don't. . .'

'Please,' Nour interrupted, her hands twisting together agitatedly. 'I'm not trying to trap you or. . .or anything but. . . Oh, Allah, be merciful, I hope you *are* Eleanor!'

# CHAPTER NINE

THE unnatural silence stretched between the two of them while Helen tried to decide what to do.

Nour would hardly have challenged her in this way if she hadn't been almost certain of her identity, but what was the reason for the air of desperation in her words?

'Yes,' she whispered fatalistically, knowing the silence had gone on too long for any credible denial.

'Oh, Allah be praised,' Nour breathed as she clenched her hands tightly together. 'You are alive! You are really here!'

Helen watched in amazement as her large dark eyes brimmed with tears, the discreetly tinted lips trembling as she tried to control her emotions.

'What happened to you?' Nour demanded in a quavering voice. 'Where have you been? We looked for you everywhere but no one could find you. . .'

Now it was Helen's turn to fight tears as she realised the terrible choice she faced.

Mahmoud had obviously lied to his family about his attempts to find his lost wife, but how could Helen tell Nour that the reason she'd had to disappear was fear that a second attempt on her life might succeed?

'Why do you look so different?' Nour demanded before Helen found her voice, and she breathed a small sigh of relief at the reprieve. 'What has happened to your face and all your beautiful hair?'

'I—I was in an accident and my face. . .' She gestured

towards her altered features with a resigned shrug. 'The surgeons did what they could to put everything back together, but somehow the jigsaw never quite looks the same the second time. . .'

'Ah, how I have missed your English humour,' Nour commented with a watery chuckle as she came round from behind her desk and embraced Helen warmly. 'How I have missed *you*, my friend,' she added as they stood together.

'How did you know she was Eleanor?' Noah's voice demanded softly as he joined them silently and pushed the office door closed behind him. 'What was it that gave her away?'

The fiercely vigilant expression on Noah's face made Nour take several steps backwards, almost as if she was afraid of what she could read in his eyes.

'P-partly it was her voice,' she began nervously. 'When I heard her talking to Nashir I recognised the way she pronounced certain words, but mostly it was the way she reacted to him. She held him as if she really loved him and it told me what I needed to know. . .'

It was Noah's arm which encircled Helen now, a clear signal to all who cared to look that she was under his protection—no longer easy prey.

'If you knew who she was last night why didn't you say something?' Noah challenged.

'Because I could see that she was frightened, and I needed to find out why before I said anything,' Nour replied simply. 'Eleanor was my friend and I would never knowingly do anything to cause her harm.'

'Unlike some members of your family,' he muttered under his breath.

He obviously hadn't spoken quietly enough because Nour pounced on his words.

'Who?' she demanded, confronting him openly. 'Who has wished Eleanor harm?'

'You are very loyal to your family,' Helen began, hoping to defuse the situation, but Nour refused to be deflected.

'Who?' she repeated adamantly.

'You mean, apart from your sister?' Noah replied before Helen had a chance to find a diplomatic way of telling her old friend what she wanted to know.

'Your sister, who agreed to lie to Helen about the fact that she was still married to Mahmoud. Your sister, who was crazy with jealousy that Helen was carrying Mahmoud's baby when she hadn't been able to and then, when Nash was so ill, turned on her and told her that her son was defective rubbish—fit only to be thrown away.'

'It was just her jealousy speaking. She was so unhappy. . .' Helen interrupted bravely when she saw how white Nour's face had gone. She'd been so careful not to tell her how awful Fatima's rages had been. . .

'And what about Mahmoud's cruelty?' Noah began again, as fierce a defender as any white knight.

'Cruelty?' Helen saw Nour's hackles rise instinctively, and she suddenly remembered that Nour had been half in love with Mahmoud herself. 'When has Mahmoud ever been cruel?' she challenged Helen. 'He was heartbroken when you disappeared!'

'So,' Noah said in a menacingly silky voice, 'am I to take it that you think it's quite acceptable behaviour for a husband to terrorise and rape his wife to force her to bear him another child just months after she's carried his first one—and while she's nearly out of her mind with worry about his heart?'

'He *didn't*! He *wouldn't*!' Nour declared passionately, looking to Helen to back her up.

Helen didn't need to say a word for Nour to realise that everything Noah had said was true. The last remaining colour drained from her face and she sank back against the support of the desk, looking utterly shaken.

'But when all this was happening—when you were so unhappy—why didn't you say something. . .anything?' she demanded brokenly.

'Because no one would have believed me,' Helen said simply. 'Especially not Ahmad. It was *his* impossible demands which drove Mahmoud. It didn't matter what he did, or how well he did it, Ahmad always cast doubt in his mind whether he'd ever be good enough to be Ahmad's successor.'

'But Mahmoud loved you,' Nour said in a last-ditch attempt to salvage some of the idealised picture she had carried in her head. 'Surely you could have talked to him. . .explained how you felt about his demands and come to some sort of compromise. . .?'

'How do you come to a compromise with someone who sends two thugs to kidnap your son and tip your car off the road in an attempt to kill you?' Noah demanded harshly.

'No. . .' Nour wailed, and Helen watched in pity as her horrified eyes searched Noah's face in a forlorn hope that he might be wrong before they travelled to Helen.

It only took one glance at her reconstructed face and disguised appearance for Nour to realise that everything they'd said was true.

'Ah, Eleanor, I'm so sorry,' she whispered as the tears finally brimmed over and fell in a steady stream down her ashen cheeks. 'How could you ever force yourself to come back to our country?'

'For Nash,' Helen supplied simply as she gripped Noah's hand for strength. 'I love my son and I had to know if he was well—I *needed* to know if he was happy. . .'

'So.' Noah's voice broke into the uneasy silence. 'Where do we go from here? Are you going to tell your family who Helen is?'

Helen watched, every nerve stretched tight as Nour's eyes travelled between the two of them.

She knew that it was all too possible that behind the façade of the modern career woman hid the same girl who had idolised Mahmoud and had longed to be his wife. A Q'rani who would have been quite happy to have been every bit as traditional as Ahmad could have wished.

'No.' Nour shook her head, the word muffled behind the fingertips which covered her trembling mouth. 'You've been hurt enough by our family. I won't say anything. I promise.'

There was a strangely subdued air amongst the members of the extended team for the rest of the day. Peter was obviously puzzled by the tension he sensed, but took Helen's hint and stayed well out of it.

Helen was worried that the uneasy atmosphere might jeopardise their effectiveness as a team in the operating theatre, but when she saw Noah conferring with Nour several hours later her spirits rose cautiously.

She'd been on her way to double-check the supply of cross-matched blood when she caught sight of the two of them speaking together and she'd paused a moment, ready to intervene if necessary.

Both of them wore very intent expressions, and she didn't dare to release the breath she was holding until she saw Noah's nod and Nour's answering attempt at a smile.

'I've decided to do Nash's operation first,' Noah announced when Helen caught up with him again.

'But. . .' Helen's heart fell a little.

She'd half hoped that, since his case had been approved, Youssef would be operated on first. If so, Nash would have had one more day at home before he had to come into hospital, and she'd been counting on spending some of that extra time with him—reading stories and playing simple games. Anything which would start to build up the links between them again.

Now there would only be tonight, and as he would be due in the hospital early in the morning for his pre-op medication she wouldn't even be able to make an excuse for him to stay up late.

She sighed her resignation, knowing that she was only being selfish. As far as Nash was concerned, the sooner the operation was done the sooner he would be well. That was what mattered most.

Maybe. . . Her mind ran on as she sorted through a new set of possibilities. Maybe there was a chance, now that Nour knew the true story of her disappearance, that she might find a way to visit her precious son. Maybe Nour would be able to send her photos as he recovered from his operation so she would be able to see how well he responded to the fact that his heart was functioning properly at last.

Her deepest secret was the one she had never dared to voice to anyone—not even Noah.

Ever since she'd concocted her plan to be part of the team which came to Q'ran it had been her secret hope that somehow she would be able to kidnap Nash herself and whisk him back to England with her.

The fact that Noah had decided to operate on Nash first

made that wild idea a complete impossibility. There was no way she could contemplate risking her son's life by forcing him to undertake such a journey so soon after major surgery.

'Ah, Helen, don't,' Noah murmured when he entered their room that night and found her curled up on their bed in tears. 'He'll be all right. You wait and see.'

'You must be fed up with me, permanently dissolving at the drop of a hat,' she sniffed, cross that she'd succumbed again. 'Only I took *this* out from its hiding place in my wash-kit, and it just set me off. . .' She held up a small furry toy.

'What is it?' Noah circled the bed and sat down beside her to inspect the creature she'd tucked back into the crook of her arm.

'It's not a what. . .it's a who. It's Mr Bear.' She smoothed his slightly bedraggled fur, knowing the chance she had taken in bringing him with her. There had been a risk that someone in the household might have caught sight of it and remembered. . .

'He's Nash's,' she whispered. 'My friend, Lisa, sent him out when Nash was born, and it was love at first sight. Unfortunately his kidnappers didn't know, and they left him behind.' She bit her lip as she looked up at him. 'He was all I had left of my little boy until joining your team gave me hope.'

When her throat closed up and it looked as though she was going to lose her battle with tears again Noah scooped her up, teddy bear and all.

She clung tightly around his neck as he carried her through to the bathroom, where he automatically reached in and set the shower running before perching himself on the side of the adjoining bath and settling her on his lap.

'Well, you've spent this evening with Nash and tucked him into bed, and tomorrow he'll be travelling into hospital with you.'

'Just as if it was a normal situation, with the child's mother accompanying him when he arrives for an operation,' she commented.

'Except most mothers have to wait outside while their children are being operated on. *You* want to have the chance to look over the surgeon's shoulder to make sure his stitching's neat enough!'

He rocked her slowly for a minute before he spoke again, his voice thoughtful.

'Nour has offered to take your place in Theatre,' he said, his dark gaze very serious as he waited for her response.

'No! She can't!' she objected immediately, suddenly frightened that Noah wanted to ban her from being with Nash. 'I'm part of the team—a trained theatre sister specialising in. . .'

'*No one* specialises in assisting at their own son's operation,' he broke in fiercely, holding her away from him by her shoulders. 'Think about Nash and how you'd feel if you froze at the wrong moment.'

Helen gazed at his face, analysing his expression, and reluctantly saw the logic of his thinking.

'Don't shut me out,' she pleaded quietly. 'I know it's something I'd never be allowed to do back in England but. . . Please. . . Only you and Nour know there's any connection between us and. . .I could just be there in Theatre while it was going on, in case there was a problem in communication with the other theatre staff. . .' She bit her lip, knowing that she was babbling and knowing that her heart was in her eyes.

'Strictly on the understanding that if I tell you to leave you will do so immediately, without questioning my decision,' Noah conceded sternly.

'But. . .'

'*Only* on that condition,' he repeated, and Helen knew that she would have to concede.

'All right,' she murmured and laid her head down on his shoulder, suddenly so tired after all the tension during the day that she couldn't even keep her eyes open.

'Hey. . .sleeping beauty.' Noah nudged her cheek with his shoulder and she murmured crossly at the disturbance. She was quite comfortable enough where she was. . .

She felt the warm breeze flow over her face as he sighed, then the world tilted and spun ever so gently until she came to rest on a soft surface and every muscle went limp.

At some stage in the night she surfaced just long enough to realise that Noah was in the bed beside her, and she burrowed trustingly into his arms before drifting off again.

'You're no fun,' a deep male voice complained in her ear as she slowly began to surface the next morning. 'I've been lying here for hours, wide awake, and all you've done is snore in my ear.'

'I do *not* snore,' Helen mumbled sleepily and began to burrow down again.

'Oh, no, you don't, my girl,' Noah said with a laugh. 'You're not going back to sleep. It's time to get up.'

'Don't want to,' she said with a pout like a sulky child, and screwed her eyes up tight.

'I can't kiss you if you bury your head like that,' Noah whispered. 'Don't you want me to kiss you good morning?'

'Mmm,' she agreed and puckered up her lips without even opening her eyes.

'Laziness, have I ever offended thee,' he laughed. 'Aren't you even going to have a look to make certain you're kissing the right person?'

Noah's gentle teasing had achieved what no alarm clock had ever managed—she was wide awake and ready for mischief just minutes after she'd first surfaced, but she wasn't going to let him know that. Not yet.

'Mmm,' she murmured, amazed at her temerity as she nuzzled her way across his chest then lapped at his skin like a cat. 'That's the right man,' she said in a voice full of satisfaction. 'He tastes right.'

At the first touch of her tongue she'd felt Noah grow tense, and she smiled secretively when she felt his less easily hidden reaction to her behaviour against the soft skin of her thigh.

'Witch,' he muttered hoarsely. 'You're beginning to make a habit of this in the morning.'

'Habit?' she murmured innocently as she finally raised drowsy eyelids to look at his sun-striped face across the narrow width of the pillow they were sharing. 'Whatever do you mean?'

'This,' he said as, with one swift movement, he flattened her in the middle of the bed and pinned her down, one of her wrists manacled in each hand as he loomed over her.

For one horrible moment Helen was taken back two years, and she felt her eyes widen with fear as the adrenaline reached her heart and it began to race.

'Oh, God!'

Helen was gazing up into his face so she saw when remembrance struck Noah and, with it, remorse.

'I'm sorry, sweetheart,' he soothed as he released her

hands and started to lift his weight off her. 'I completely forgot. . .'

'Stay. . .' Helen whispered, shocking herself nearly as much as she surprised Noah.

'What?' He froze. 'Are you sure?' His eyes were gazing intently into hers at short range, their faces no more than a few inches apart.

'I'm certain,' she said huskily as she used her freedom to slide her arms around him. 'For a long time I was afraid that I'd never be able to forget the horror—never be able to allow a man to put me in a position of vulnerability to make love.'

'And now?' he prompted, staying absolutely still while she tentatively explored the purely pleasurable sensations of having a man lying on top of her, his aroused body making a space for itself between her thighs.

'Now I think that, with the right man, this is something I could definitely grow to like. . .'

The whispered avowal was cut off by the sharp bleep as Noah's alarm clock went off, and they both realised with a sudden jolt that today was not a day when either of them wanted to be late.

'Nash's operation,' Helen said in a stricken whisper. 'I was going to be with him when he woke up this morning and read him a story to take his mind off the fact that he can't have anything to eat.'

'I'm sure that Nour will have made certain he's not breaking his fast,' Noah reassured her as she scrambled out from under his weight, nearly tumbling him to the floor in her hurry to get to the bathroom.

'You don't understand,' she whispered harshly, ever mindful that she might be overheard but almost frantic at the thought of the lost minutes. 'Because Youssef is being operated on too we'll be here a bit longer, but once he's stabilised we'll be going and I won't be able to see Nash any more until...until who knows when!'

'Calm down,' Noah soothed as he followed her into the bathroom and shut the door behind them, but she was too het up to listen.

She hadn't realised that he'd waited just long enough for her to step into the shower before he caught her unawares, by wrapping his big body around hers.

'Calm down,' he repeated as he ran his hands soothingly up and down her arms.

'Calm down? You're telling me to calm down? How *can* I calm down when I'm going to be watching my little boy have a major operation on his heart in just a few hours...?'

'Sweetheart, if you *don't* calm down you're not even going to be allowed inside the operating theatre!'

Helen stared up at Noah with her mouth open, not even noticing, in her shock that the shower water was falling inside. She'd never heard him speak like that before; never realised how stern he could be if someone fell short of his expectations.

Suddenly she realised just what she must have sounded like as she ranted at him and, although she knew that her nervousness was understandable, to let it get the better of her in that way when she was supposed to be a health-care professional was inexcusable.

'I'm sorry,' she whispered, hanging her head and so ashamed by her loss of control that she couldn't look him in the eye. 'I promise that will never happen again.'

'I know it won't,' Noah said with a wealth of understanding in his voice as he wrapped his arms around her again. 'I've worked with you long enough at the hospital to know that you're an excellent nurse, and over the last few weeks I've come to know you well enough as a person to realise that this was an isolated incident brought on by stress.'

Helen sagged against him, held up only by the circle of his arms as she drew in a shuddering breath.

'*Are* you going to ban me from Theatre?' she asked in a very small voice.

'I don't think it will be necessary,' he reassured her with a smile as he smoothed the wet tendrils of hair away from her face. 'In fact, I hope you *are* there because we've begun to work very well as a team and you'll be able to clarify any problems with our host colleagues—now that I've got you house-trained.'

'Huh! I'm not a leaky puppy, you know,' she retorted with a spark of her old fire. 'I'm a top notch theatre sister!'

'Who just happens to have the sexiest body I've ever seen on a theatre sister,' he growled as he pretended to bite the side of her neck. 'But if she doesn't shift her curvy butt out of this shower in the next five seconds that sexy body is going to be responsible for wrecking the team's reputation for punctuality!'

She squealed as he aimed a swat at the portion of her anatomy in question and she retaliated by switching the shower to cold water, making her own escape before the icy deluge descended.

Helen was stealing a few extra minutes with Nash when she saw Nour catch up with Noah. She was too far away to hear what they were saying but their expressions told her that it was serious.

She hurried through towards the operating theatre, worried that something had gone wrong, but before she could ask him what they'd been talking about Noah asked her to spend some time with Youssef's family.

'I know there are other people better qualified to speak their language,' he said when she began to remonstrate with him—*she* wanted to be the one to give Nash his pre-med and stay with him when he went down to Theatre.

'I think they'd appreciate talking to someone who's part of a team which regularly performs this type of surgery,' Noah continued, ignoring her attempts to interrupt. 'You'll be able to relate to their worries the way no one else can.'

As she sat and spoke to the young couple Helen had to admit that he'd had a point, as Youssef's parents were desperately grateful for any little snippet of comfort she could give them.

At one point they seemed to be talking at cross-purposes as to when their son was being operated on, but Helen put that down to a combination of her imperfect Arabic and her lack of concentration as she kept glancing at the clock.

Part of her wanted to scream at the delay, wondering what was going wrong that she hadn't been called to accompany Nash into Theatre. She knew that Nour was a more familiar face to him, but her mother's instinct was strong enough that *she* wanted to be there to hold his little hand.

'Excuse me, please.' The softly spoken words came from the young Arabic nurse at her elbow.

'Nour has sent me to apologise for the delay, and to ask if you would like to go to Theatre now. The operation has started, and I will stay here with Youssef's family.'

Helen looked up into the smooth perfection of her olive-toned face, her large dark eyes calm and open, and suddenly she knew that something wasn't right.

Barely remembering to wish the young couple a polite

farewell, she took off at a brisk walk—her pulse racing with fear as she hurried through to the theatre suite and gowned up. She had so wanted to be with Nash; to have been able to reassure him. . . And, because of some sort of delay, she'd missed her chance. . .

When she pushed her way through the doors and entered the brightly lit room Noah looked up as if he'd been waiting for her to appear, his expression hidden by the high-tech operating microscope already in position in front of his eyes and the mask covering the lower half of his face.

'Everything all right?' he called, just loudly enough so that his voice carried over the sound of all the complicated monitoring equipment.

'Fine,' she replied, hoping that her mask muffled her voice enough to hide the tremor which had assailed her as soon as she saw the precious little body already opened to Noah's intent gaze.

In accordance with their agreement, she stayed well back against the wall—just a couple of steps inside the room.

In spite of the fact that his Q'rani opposite number was an unusually tall man for his nationality there had been no doubt in Helen's mind as to which of the figures around the table was Noah, even if he hadn't spoken to her, and her eyes were riveted to the broad-shouldered man dressed in the ubiquitous shapeless theatre pyjamas.

Until she'd been introduced to him Helen had been worried that Saud Rafat might have resented Noah's presence, but he'd been openly delighted to have the chance to assist a surgeon of Noah's calibre and was proud to tell them of the extra training he'd undertaken in America.

'How's it going your end, Pete?' she heard Noah ask

and she found herself standing a little straighter, even leaning forward, as she waited for the reply.

'Everything's going well,' Peter reported. 'How about yours?'

'Ditto,' he replied in their usual shorthand. 'Ready to put him on bypass? I'm repairing the ventricular septal defect first. . . Time?'

Helen found herself crossing her fingers surreptitiously.

She knew, without having to listen to Noah's running commentary, that the team had now completed the initial preparatory work and were ready for the machines to take over the job of keeping the circulation going while the first of the heart defects was repaired.

She didn't need to be looking over Noah's shoulder to know that he was starting with the open-heart part of the process, and that he was going to have to suture a precisely tailored Gore-Tex patch over the hole between the two upper chambers of the heart.

When he straightened up and uttered a restrained, 'Lovely,' she felt as if she was drawing her first full breath in hours.

She didn't really feel as though she could believe that everything was going well until Noah looked towards her and deliberately caught her worried gaze. It was only because she had come to know him so well over the last few days that she was able to tell, from the little she could see of him, that he was smiling at her as he rotated each shoulder to loosen the muscles.

As he stepped forward again to begin the next stage she couldn't help an answering smile when she heard Peter's familiar comment, 'Seconds out for round two!'

'What did he say?' muttered the most junior of the nurses, and Helen was distracted for a moment while she discovered how difficult it was to translate a joke into another language.

By the time she turned her attention back to the table Noah had already started to correct the obstruction to the blood flow out of the right ventricle of the heart.

Time ceased to have any meaning as she followed every stage of the complicated operation, her ears always attuned to Peter's periodic reports on their little patient's vital signs—the slightest arrhythmia in the electronic beeps of the monitoring equipment enough to stop her own heart beating.

When the original temporary shunt was finally removed and it was time to allow the blood to flow back into the heart Helen was so tense that she felt as if the slightest thing would make her shatter into a thousand pieces.

She found herself holding her breath as she waited for Noah's voice to confirm the success of the operation, but after his report that the heart had grown pink the steady electronic rhythm faltered.

'We've got a problem.' Professionalism kept Peter's voice calm, in spite of the warning screams his machinery was emitting.

'No leaks anywhere,' Noah confirmed, his blood-covered hands hovering over the gaping wound in the little chest. 'But no spontaneous heartbeat. Paddles,' he demanded decisively. 'Quickly!'

Helen only just stopped herself from rushing forward to hand him the paddles herself, her own heart pounding frantically as her eyes flicked rapidly from the inexorably ticking clock on the wall to the rapid activity taking place around the little body.

It seemed to take for ever for the paddles to be placed on either side of the exposed heart and a measured jolt of electricity passed between them, but the suddenly renewed rhythmic bleeping of the monitor was greeted with an open cheer by the whole team.

'Thank God,' Helen whispered as she sagged back against the wall, her forehead clammy with the sweat of terror which had covered her when she thought she had watched Nash die on the operating table. 'Oh, thank you, God. . .' She concentrated on drawing slow steady breaths to stop herself collapsing in an undignified heap.

Finally Noah finished closing the enormous wound, and Helen watched as he straightened up to his full height and shrugged to relieve the tension.

' ''That's all, folks,'' ' he quoted as he turned to Peter one last time. 'Are you happy up there?'

'Delighted,' Peter confirmed from his position above the head of the table as their little patient was prepared for transfer to Recovery. 'Everything now within normal parameters. My compliments.'

His heavy-handed brogue drew a shaky smile from Helen. That told her, as nothing else would, that the two of them were satisfied with the way everything had turned out.

Now all she had to do was wait while Nash began his recovery, and hope that they were in Q'ran long enough for her to spend some more time with him.

# CHAPTER TEN

'No! WE *can't*. Not yet!' Helen's heart was pounding and her hands had begun to shake as she paced backwards and forwards in their little borrowed office. She'd had no idea why Noah had wanted to speak to her in private, but she would never have guessed that it could be *this*.

'Helen,' Noah began persuasively, 'Saud is perfectly capable of supervising a post-operative patient. He's an extremely good surgeon.'

'But I want it to be *you* looking after him,' she pleaded. 'I *know* you. I *trust* you. . .'

'Then trust me to do the right thing,' he countered gently, his voice so calm that she felt like screaming.

'But you haven't even done Youssef's surgery. Ahmad is going to pay all the expenses for you to do it.' She was clutching at straws now, and she knew it.

'I've already indicated to the hospital authorities that I'm willing to take Youssef back to England with us and carry out his surgery there. I offered to pay all his travelling and hospital expenses myself.'

'But. . .'

'The authorities have started processing some sort of emergency paperwork to allow him to travel out with us this evening.'

'This evening! But. . .'

'Please, Helen,' he interrupted, 'Don't make this any more traumatic than it has to be. You know only too well

171

that when I get a call like this I have to go. A life could be at stake.'

Helen subsided. When it came down to basics she didn't really have a case to argue. If a call had come through that Noah's skill was needed urgently elsewhere. . .

'And I suppose there's no way I could stay on for a few days?' she said sadly as she mentally added up the precious minutes she'd been able to spend beside her unconscious child. There had been so many tubes and monitors attached to his little body that if she hadn't known who he was she'd never have recognised him.

'You're an essential part of the team—my right arm in an unknown operating theatre. The situation here was a one-off. I can't take the chance that someone who doesn't know my methods will falter at a critical moment.'

Helen sighed shakily and resigned herself unwillingly to the fact that she was going to have to leave Q'ran with the rest of the team. By the time it grew dark tonight she would be airborne, and flying further and further away from Nash.

'Oh, Noah,' she murmured miserably and walked into his welcoming embrace. 'It took me so long to get here and I've seen so little of him.'

'Oh, Helen,' he sighed and tightened his arms around her. 'Trust me. Nash is going to be fine.'

Helen felt the gentle kiss he brushed over her hair, and her heart was filled with a confusing jumble of emotions. One part of her was mourning the fact that she was going to be separated from her precious son again, this time *knowing* that he wasn't happy.

At the same time her growing attraction to Noah and her responsiveness to his every word and gesture was making her wonder if she wasn't committing the most hazardous of mistakes—falling in love with him.

Slowly she forced herself to leave the comfort of his embrace.

They had entered into their marriage of convenience at his suggestion, but it had only been a ploy so that she would have the chance to see her son in safety.

Soon—so much sooner than she had anticipated—they would be in England again, and while her new name would probably mean that she didn't have to worry about looking over her shoulder, it also meant that there would be no need for the two of them to continue the charade.

'I'd better go and see what needs doing to make Youssef's transfer to the airport go smoothly,' she said, her voice flat as she began to realise just how much she was going to miss the two men in her life. The future was going to seem very flat and grey. . .

'You don't have to worry about that,' Noah informed her easily. 'Nour is taking care of it.'

He sounded so calm, she thought in amazement. Didn't he *ever* let his emotions get the better of him?

'She suggested that you might like to go back to Ahmad's house to get everything packed up,' Noah continued as he tapped a pile of notes together and slid them into his briefcase.

'In that case, I'll just go up and spend a few minutes with Nash,' she said in a strained voice, her heart feeling as if it was being squeezed by a giant fist.

'I'm afraid there won't be time for that.' He cast a fleeting glance at the slim watch on his wrist. 'The car should be here in about five minutes.'

Helen stopped dead in her tracks, her breath frozen in her throat and her eyes burning with the threat of tears.

'I see.' Her teeth were gritted as she fought for control,

and she had to force the words out. 'What time will you be coming to the house?'

'I won't,' he said shortly. 'I'll stay here to keep an eye on Nash—and Youssef—until the last minute. Peter will be coming back to collect his belongings later on, but I'll travel straight to the airport with our patient and meet you there.'

'So you want me to do your packing too?'

'That sounds like a nice wifely gesture,' he teased gently, but the joke fell on stony ground.

'Don't get too attached to the idea,' she reminded him, her unhappiness making her delivery curt. 'Our arrangement will be ending soon.'

If she hadn't been looking straight at him she wouldn't have seen the sudden change in Noah's expression. For just a fraction of a second it seemed as if she had hurt him in some way, but by the time she looked again he had drawn down the shutters and was as impassive as ever.

As she made her way out of the air-conditioned comfort of the hospital, and braved the searing heat to walk out to the waiting limousine, she wished that she had just a little of Noah's impressive control. She was certain that her soul-deep unhappiness must be as easily read on her face as words on the page of an open book.

It wasn't until she'd arrived outside Ahmad bin Ali's house that she realised that she was going to be responsible for delivering the team's thanks for Ahmad's hospitality, and she couldn't help the shiver of fear which snaked its way up her spine.

She'd managed to avoid him as much as possible throughout their stay, but common politeness dictated that she couldn't leave without observing the courtesies.

The coward inside her made her put off the evil hour as she hurried through the cool of the house to the room she and Noah had been using.

In spite of the fact that they had been sharing a bed for several weeks now, and she had even touched him with a degree of intimacy, it still felt strange to be handling his personal effects and packing them neatly away in his suitcase.

When she caught herself lifting his soap to her nose to breathe in the familiar smell she gave an exclamation of disgust at her idiocy and thrust it into his wash-bag.

Honestly, she lectured herself as she finished the task in record time, she was behaving no better than some silly hormone-driven teenager mooning over her favourite film star. She had more important things to do.

Packing her own wash-bag was a different matter.

She'd bought the big squashy bag deliberately so that there would be room for her to hide Mr Bear in the bottom. Even when she was contemplating how dangerous it could be if someone in Ahmad's household had recognised the familiar toy she'd hoped that, by covering him with layers of make-up and the usual female sanitary requirements, anyone nosy enough to look inside wouldn't bother delving too far.

Now she was faced with a decision.

She'd known that Nash had been very attached to Mr Bear, and she had been delighted to discover during their all too brief time together that he still remembered him. She stood in the silence of the bathroom she'd designed so long ago, stroking Mr Bear's soft furry body and weighing up her options.

Should she leave the toy behind, trusting Nour to find some way of letting Nash have his little friend without arousing suspicion? Or should she take him back with her again so that she would still have one small link with the baby she'd lost?

With a catch in her breath she pushed the little creature to the bottom of the bag and piled her belongings in on top. She had no idea how long it was going to be before she could see Nash again, and she was going to need something to hold onto—especially as she was going to be losing Noah too.

Once the suitcases were neatly stacked beside the door in readiness for her departure, Helen drew in a steadying breath and went towards the courtyard garden in search of Ahmad.

Her heart sank when the first person she came across was Fatima. For a moment she paused in the archway and nearly gave in to the temptation to disappear again before Fatima noticed her and try again later, but at the last moment she stopped and straightened her shoulders in determination.

She wasn't going to let the bad memories of this house and its inhabitants rule her life any more.

'I'm sorry to disturb you,' she began politely as she stepped into the colourful oasis. 'I'm looking for Mr bin Ali.'

'What you want 'im for?' Fatima demanded harshly, her dark eyes filled with burning animosity and all the meekness she pretended to in the presence of the men of the house gone without trace. 'He too busy to see you.'

Helen had stiffened reflexively when she found herself on the receiving end of Fatima's sharp tongue once more, but she felt the colour drain away from her face completely when she heard the coarse Arabic epithet which was added to the English.

She'd heard that word and many like it in the time that she'd shared a house with this bitter woman.

'I realise he's a busy man,' she said in a conciliatory tone, making the effort to keep her voice quietly even, 'but I want to thank him, on behalf of the team, for inviting us into his home.'

'Is not necessary,' she spat dismissively. 'I tell 'im you go. More better you not come to Q'ran. . .' She lapsed into strangely disjointed Arabic.

Helen listened in amazement as she struggled to make sense of her translation.

'He not need doctor. . . Not need hospital. . . Should be dead like woman whose blood he carries. . . Fools. . .! I told them. . .I told them. . . Why they only kill her. . .? Why bring baby with sick heart. . .?'

Helen nearly gasped aloud with shock when she realised what she was hearing, and quietly stepped back out into the dimness of the corridor without attracting Fatima's attention.

As she hurried towards her room her thoughts were whirling frantically around in her head.

Was the woman mad? Even allowing for Helen's less than accurate translation, it sounded as if it had been *Fatima* who had been responsible for the attempt on her life—for killing her friend, Lisa.

Helen locked the door and perched herself on the edge of the bed, wrapping her arms around herself in a defensive way and terrified that she was going to fall apart.

What was she going to do now?

How could she fly back to England with Noah, knowing that as soon as he was well enough to come home from hospital Nash was going to be returning to the home of the woman who had tried to have him killed?

She couldn't!

She just *couldn't* leave her son to return to this danger!

Distraught, she rocked herself backwards and forwards while she tried to decide what to do.

Should she wait for Peter to come and give him a message for Noah? Should she give him Noah's belongings to deliver and find herself somewhere near the hospital to stay until Nash was well enough to leave—well enough to travel?

Finally she arrived at the only real solution—she would have to tell Noah herself.

When she took the cases to the airport she would have to tell him what she'd found out. He was sure to know what to do. He would understand why she had to stay— why she couldn't leave her son to be a victim of Fatima's hatred.

It seemed as if days had passed by the time she finally heard Peter's cheery greeting as he passed her door on the way to his own room.

'Car's ready and waiting, me darlin'. Stir your stumps,' he called as he beat out a musical tattoo on the door in passing.

'Thank God,' Helen breathed, grateful that at least the waiting was over. There was no way she wanted to encounter Fatima again.

She stood just behind the door until she heard Peter's returning footsteps, then swung the door open.

'Have you got a spare hand?' she asked with a deliberate attempt at cheerfulness. 'Noah left me to pack his things, but I can't manage to carry all the cases at once.'

'No problem, light of my life,' he teased. 'For the price of one smile I'd carry your suitcase to the ends of the earth.'

'Just out to the car will be far enough,' she said drily, but his nonsense had been just what she needed.

'Did you see our gracious host?' Peter enquired as they crossed the entrance hall for the last time and he cast a lingering look towards the archway and the wonderful courtyard.

'Apparently he was too busy to see me, but I asked Fatima to pass on our thanks for his hospitality.'

Even though she had given a much-edited version of their meeting just the memory of it was enough to start her hands trembling again.

'I'm sure Noah will send an official letter on behalf of the team once we return to England—just to make sure Ahmad doesn't get left with the feeling that we were too casual about the whole thing.'

The bags were stacked neatly in the boot of the gleaming vehicle when Helen hurried into the cool interior. It wasn't the heat that was driving her but the fear that something might happen at the last minute to jog Fatima's memory, or that they might not get to the airport in time for her to explain the new situation to Noah.

Peter filled the short journey with his usual brand of entertaining chat, pointing out the interesting and the unusual as they passed through this almost barren region of the world, but Helen hardly heard a word.

Her eyes were concentrating on the sweep-hand of her watch as it crawled its way round the dial and her mind was repeating over and over the single word, *hurry*.

'Here we are, me darlin',' Peter announced as the car turned in through the well-signposted gateway, his voice finally breaking through the fog of agitation that surrounded her. 'Next stop England where, in spite of the fact that it's supposed to be summer, the rain will probably be tippin' down!'

And I wouldn't mind a bit—if I was taking Nash safely home with me, she thought in anguish.

As soon as the car stopped she was out, for once not even noticing the heat beating down on her as she retrieved the luggage from the boot and set off in the direction of the airport buildings.

'Peter. . .!' a familiar voice called and the two of them turned to see Noah, standing at another entrance. 'This way,' he said as he beckoned them, then continued when they drew closer, 'You've just got time to have your luggage weighed and checked and your passports stamped. The flight has got an earlier departure slot than we expected.'

'No. . .!' Helen breathed in despair, her feet refusing to move another step while she tried to cope with yet another setback to her plans.

'Noah,' she called agitatedly, 'I need to speak to you for a minute, please.'

'I'm sorry, Helen, there isn't time. It'll have to wait until we're airborne.'

'But it can't. . .' she began to wail as she hurried to keep up with their much longer legs, but no one was listening. The whole world seemed to be scurrying about as busily as ants, as the final passengers were boarding and their luggage was loaded.

In a terrible daze Helen watched as her passport was stamped and her suitcase was weighed. She only just had the presence of mind to retrieve her hand luggage, clutching it in her arms when she remembered the precious toy it contained.

As if sleepwalking, she allowed herself to be led along

the ramp and in through the rear entrance of the plane to the place where their patient waited for them.

'Nour. . .?' Helen questioned blankly when she recognised the young woman beside the travelling stretcher.

'Hello, Eleanor. I travelled with our patient so I would have a chance to say goodbye to you.' She flung her arms around Helen's shoulders, apparently unaware that Helen was slow to respond. 'Take care of yourself. I hope one day I will be able to visit you in England.'

'Take care of yourself, Nour.' Helen returned the words by rote, but suddenly their meaning registered and she gripped Nour's hands fiercely. 'Look after Nash for me, Nour. Please! Don't let anyone harm him. . .'

Before she could say any more the stewardess was requesting that the passengers take their seats, and Nour had to go.

'Goodbye, Nour,' Helen called as the young woman reached the exit. 'Remember. . .'

In the flurry of checking their little patient's oxygen mask and settling themselves into their seats there was no time for further regrets. It wasn't until the plane had actually taken off and was climbing powerfully into the sky that the solution occurred to her.

'I could go back,' she whispered under her breath as she watched the stony, arid land recede under the plane's wings. 'As soon as Youssef has had his operation I could fly back and still be here in time for Nash to come out.'

'What was that?' Noah leant towards her with a slight frown on his face. 'Did you say something, Helen?'

She started to shake her head, then paused. They might be surrounded by other people but, with the plane still climbing, the noise was great enough for few of them to be able to overhear her voice—and, anyway, there wasn't the same need for secrecy which had accompanied their outward journey.

'Noah, I've decided to hand in my resignation,' she said quietly, and watched in surprise as the shock of the announcement robbed his face of colour.

'Why?' he demanded.

'Because as soon as Youssef's had his operation I'm going back to Q'ran. I can't bear to leave Nash in that terrible house. I know he isn't safe, but most of all I know he isn't loved.'

'Oh, Helen,' he said as he captured one hand in both of his. 'Calm down a minute and let me tell you what. . .'

'No, Noah,' she interrupted in a fierce whisper. 'There's no point in trying to persuade me. I've made up my mind.'

'Helen, please let me. . .'

'Noah, I can't let him. . . Oh. . .!'

Suddenly she couldn't speak any more; couldn't even breathe as Noah cupped her face between his hands and kissed her, thoroughly. . .endlessly. . .

'What. . .?' Helen gasped when he finally let her up for air.

'Just shut up a minute and let me speak, will you, woman?' he growled. 'Or I'll be forced to do that again!'

Helen didn't know whether to glare at him for his display of blatant chauvinism or beg him to repeat the delicious punishment, so she subsided weakly.

'Your resignation is not acceptable,' he began sternly. 'And you won't be going back to Q'ran any time in the near future—you're going to have far too many responsibilities in England.'

'But you don't understand,' she pleaded helplessly. 'I've got to go back to keep Nash safe. . .'

'Where's that enormous wash bag of yours?' Noah
demanded, completely cutting across what she was trying to say.

'It's by my feet,' she said with a distracted wave of her
hand in the direction of the space under the seat in front.
'But, Noah, you *must* listen to me. . .'

'Pass it to me, please,' he requested politely, and she
was so nonplussed that she did as he asked, handing him
the hand luggage which contained the bag in question and
then watching in bemusement as he delved inside.

'Is this the one?' He pulled out the squashy water-
proof bag.

'Yes.' She was totally confused now.

'And if I remember rightly,' he murmured as he slid
his hand down through the jumbled contents, 'right at the
bottom. . . Ah!' He made a satisfied sound as he drew out
his prize. 'Mr Bear himself,' he said triumphantly, and
glanced towards the sign before he released his seat belt.

'Noah?' She was more bewildered than ever. 'What do
you want Mr Bear for? Where are you taking him. . .?'

She released her own seat belt and slid across to watch
as Noah took the precious toy across the narrow gangway
to the specially angled stretcher locked in position under
the window the other side.

'Hello,' she heard him say softly to their small patient.
'I've got a little friend I'd like you to meet.'

Helen watched in puzzlement as he held up the slightly
bedraggled toy, but even through the distortion of the
oxygen mask she heard the little voice.

'Mr Bear.' His dark eyes opened wide and Helen
watched with tears in her eyes as amazement turned to
joy. 'It's my Mr Bear,' the little voice repeated as he held
out both hands for his long-lost favourite.

Between one heartbeat and the next Helen was out of her seat and crouching beside her precious child, unable to prevent the tears of happiness pouring down her face as she confirmed that their patient really *was* her son.

She was still fighting a losing battle with tears when Noah finally persuaded her to return to her seat. He pushed the dividing armrest out of the way and gathered her up in his arms.

'It's Nash,' she told him, totally unnecessarily. 'I don't know what's going on, but that's my little boy,' she said and flung her arms round Noah's neck.

'*Now* are you ready to listen?' he said with a teasing and long-suffering air.

'Please. . .tell me how you worked such a miracle,' she said, and buried her tearful face in the angle of his neck.

'It was Nour's idea initially,' he began as he handed her a large white handkerchief. 'As soon as she found out what had really happened to you she was worried that Nash could still be in danger. She came to me and suggested we should swap the two children over.'

'But,' Helen objected, 'she couldn't have known that you were going to get a call to come back to England. . . Oh! Was that *your* contribution to the plot?'

He nodded, and she let his deep voice flow over her as he told her how Nour had exchanged the wristbands and medical notes on their two little patients just long enough to have the documentation organised for Nash's travel permits, then made certain that Youssef and his notes were reunited for the rest of his stay in hospital.

'So Youssef's parents *were* right when they thought he was having surgery,' she mused, remembering the confusion. 'But why didn't you tell me what was going on? It would have saved me all the worry. . .'

'The fewer people who knew the better,' Noah said wisely. 'We couldn't afford for you to give the game away by spending too much time with someone else's child at the wrong moment.'

'But. . .'

'Don't you think this is a case when all's well that ends well?' he suggested softly, his dark blue eyes wearing a gentle expression as they gazed down at her.

Helen's heart turned over. Why did she have to remember now, when she wanted to surround herself with happiness, that she might have one of her men safely with her but she would be losing the other one as soon as he could arrange the annulment.

'What have you thought of now?' he demanded, cradling her chin and bringing her eyes up to meet his when she would have looked away.

'I was only. . . What will happen when Mahmoud finds out where Nash has gone?' she asked on an inspiration, hoping to sidetrack him.

'Nour has no doubts that she will be able to sort that end of things out, especially as she knows the *real* story of what happened. As Nash is the child of a bigamous marriage it all but destroys Mahmoud's claim to him. Now, tell me what you were worrying about.'

Helen was surprised how little that shaming word meant to her with Noah seated beside her, but she should have remembered that he was too persistent to fall for simple diversions.

'I was just wondering. . .' she began, trying to find a roundabout way of asking what she wanted to know, then opting for the direct approach. 'What's going to happen to us?' she said simply.

'That depends,' Noah said, and her heart began to sink.

'On what?' she asked in a small voice.

'On whether you think you could put up with me on a long-term basis,' he suggested, and it was the darkening hue of his cheeks which gave Helen the courage to hope.

'Long-term?' she enquired innocently. 'How long?'

'Well, if you weren't in love with a person I suppose a lifetime together could seem like a very long time, but if you think you could manage to fall in love with a heart surgeon with a rather battered heart. . .'

'Then a lifetime wouldn't be long-term enough,' she supplied when he ran out of words, and cradled his face between her hands. 'Oh, Noah, I think I've been falling in love with you for weeks—ever since you took my breath away by proposing.'

'Well, it was about time,' he grumbled as he wrapped his arms tightly around her. 'I think I began to fall in love with you when you first joined the staff at St Augustine's, but I wasn't absolutely certain until Nour showed me a photo of you with your natural colouring. I've always had a special liking for curvaceous blondes with a river of hair flowing right down their back. . .'

'Beast!' she pouted. 'For a minute I thought you really meant it when you said you'd fallen for me months ago.'

'But I did,' he said quietly. 'I fell in love with your sweetness and your gentle nature and the love you give to every one of your little charges, and all I wanted was for you to love me the same way.'

'Oh, Noah,' Helen breathed. 'I *do* love you. So much that the thought of our marriage being annulled was like having my heart ripped out.'

There was a long silence as he tried to reassure her with a kiss that she would never have to worry about her heart again, and they had both surfaced with unsteady breathing and racing hearts when Noah started to chuckle.

'What?' Helen demanded when she saw the wicked twinkle in his eyes.

'Oh, it was just a stray thought,' he said airily.

'Tell me about it,' she invited, intrigued by the boyish grin which he couldn't control.

'Well, I've been dreaming about making love to you for over half a year and I've been married to you for a month and I still haven't had my dreams come true.'

'Well, Mr Heart Surgeon,' she whispered with a husky chuckle of her own and a beckoning finger. 'I think we can safely say that tonight is the night that all our dreams will come true!'

MILLS & BOON®

*Medical Romance*™

# COMING NEXT MONTH

## NOT HUSBAND MATERIAL! by Caroline Anderson
*Audley Memorial Hospital*

Jill Craig was not impressed when the flirtatious, but very handsome Zach Samuels breezed into the Audley and proceeded to charm everyone—including herself! She could not deny the intense desire that they both felt, but could she trust him to love only her?

## A CAUTIOUS LOVING by Margaret O'Neill

Dr Thomas Brodie was reluctant to hire Miranda Gibbs. Why was such a beautiful, intelligent and diligent woman moving to the country? But then he saw her in action as a nurse. Miranda might get the job but she would never have his heart...

## WINGS OF SPIRIT by Meredith Webber
*Flying Doctors*

Christa Cassimatis had known station owner Andrew Walsh on a strictly professional basis for months, so she was astonished when Andrew suddenly proposed! She barely knew the man, and now he wanted to get married! She knew it must be for all the wrong reasons...

## PRESTON'S PRACTICE by Carol Wood

The name Preston Lynley rang alarm bells for Vanessa Perry! But then Preston provoked the most surprising reactions, including being incredibly attracted to him, from the minute she had begun her new job at his Medical Practice! But he also made Vanessa remember her tragic past—and his link to it...

# MILLS & BOON®

*Medical Romance™*

# Flying Doctors

Don't miss this exciting new mini-series from popular
Medical Romance author, Meredith Webber.

**Set in the heat of the Australian outback,
the Flying Doctor mini-series experiences
the thrills, drama and romance of life
on a flying doctor station.**

**Look out for:**

Wings of Spirit by Meredith Webber
in June '97

New York Times bestselling author

# JAYNE ANN KRENTZ

## *Full Bloom*

Part bodyguard, part troubleshooter, Jacob Stone
had, over the years, pulled Emily out of countless
acts of rebellion against her domineering family.
Now he'd been summoned to rescue her from a
disastrous marriage. Emily didn't want his
protection—she needed his love. But did Jacob
need this new kind of trouble?

*"A master of the genre...nobody does it better!"*

—Romantic Times

**AVAILABLE IN PAPERBACK
FROM MAY 1997**

# FREE!

## FOUR FREE
### specially selected
### Medical Romance™ novels
### <u>PLUS</u> a FREE Mystery Gift
### when you return this page...

Return this coupon and we'll send you 4 Medical Romance novels and a mystery gift absolutely FREE! We'll even pay the postage and packing for you.

We're making you this offer to introduce you to the benefits of the Reader Service™– FREE home delivery of brand-new Medical Romance novels, at least a month before they are available in the shops, FREE gifts and a monthly Newsletter packed with information, competitions, author profiles and lots more...

Accepting these FREE books and gift places you under no obligation to buy, you may cancel at any time, even after receiving just your free shipment. Simply complete the coupon below and send it to:

MILLS & BOON READER SERVICE, FREEPOST, CROYDON, SURREY, CR9 3WZ.

READERS IN EIRE PLEASE SEND COUPON TO PO BOX 4546, DUBLIN 24

## NO STAMP NEEDED

Yes, please send me 4 free Medical Romance novels and a mystery gift. I understand that unless you hear from me, I will receive 4 superb new titles every month for just £2.20* each, postage and packing free. I am under no obligation to purchase any books and I may cancel or suspend my subscription at any time, but the free books and gift will be mine to keep in any case. (I am over 18 years of age)

M7XE

Ms/Mrs/Miss/Mr_____
BLOCK CAPS PLEASE

Address_____

_____

_____ Postcode _____

NEW YORK TIMES
BESTSELING AUTHOR

# *Anne* Mather

## Dangerous Temptation

**He was desperate to remember...**Jake wasn't
sure why he'd agreed to take his twin brother's
place on the flight to London. But when he
awakens in hospital after the crash, he can't even
remember his own name or the beautiful woman
who watches him so guardedly. Caitlin. His wife.

**She was desperate to forget...**
Her husband seems like a stranger to Caitlin—a
man who assumes there is love when none exists.
He is totally different—like the man she'd thought
she had married. Until his memory returns.
And with it, a danger that threatens them all.

*"Ms. Mather has penned a wonderful romance."*
—Romantic Times

**MIRA®**

## AVAILABLE IN PAPERBACK
## FROM MAY 1997